A FOULED-
UP FOURTH

LARGE PRINT EDITION

ALSO BY ALEKSA BAXTER

MAGGIE MAY AND MISS FANCYPANTS MYSTERIES

A Dead Man and Doggie Delights

A Crazy Cat Lady and Canine Crunchies

A Buried Body and Barkery Bites

A Missing Mom and Mutt Munchies

A Sabotaged Celebration and Salmon Snaps

A Poisoned Past and Puppermints

***

A Fouled-Up Fourth

NOSY NEWFIE HOLIDAY SHORTS

Halloween at the Baker Valley Barkery & Cafe

A Housebound Holiday

A FOULED-UP FOURTH

A MAGGIE MAY AND MISS FANCYPANTS MYSTERY

ALEKSA BAXTER

CHAPTER 1

July first and the good news was that the valley was still safe and walled off from a country that seemed increasingly bent on following the worst possible timeline. Bad news was that gave me more time to notice who my neighbors were.

Not my grandpa, he was great. Except for the small frown he gave Matt's and my front yard whenever we forgot to mow to his satisfaction. (A small frown that turned into pointed comments about how a man's home is a reflection on him and how much he values his neighbors.)

That I could handle. I'd spent a lifetime letting subtle critiques wash off without leaving a trace.

No, it was the other neighbor I was ready to murder: Lucas Dean.

I might have been able to forget his predilection for chasing any female he legally could get away with chasing. Or his inordinate fondness for hanging out in his yard in nothing but shorts so small they belonged in the 70's. And I could have maybe even forgotten his unfortunate habit of calling me Sunshine.

(I'm pretty sure half the time he didn't remember my name. I was tempted to wear a name tag around with M-A-G-G-I-E written on it in all capital letters until he got the point, but I resisted.)

What I couldn't forget, or forgive, was his apparent fondness for fireworks. And his complete obliviousness to how much those fireworks affected poor Fancy, my four-year-old Newfoundland.

I mean, picture it. There we were, sitting in our backyard in the shadow of a pine tree, hidden away behind a six-foot fence, me reading a book, Fancy snoring away, her foot just barely touching my leg, minding our own business, enjoying the day, relaxing in the almost but not quite uncomfortable heat, and suddenly...

BOOM.

A loud banging noise from next door and then a scatter of little explosions in the air.

Fancy, poor thing, jumped to her feet, furiously barking and looking for the culprit. How dare something disturb her sleep? How dare that loud noise go off and wake her? Where was it?

She ran around the yard, barking as loud as she could, demanding answers.

"Calm down, Fancy," I said quietly, as I slowly stood up.

(I don't believe in yelling at a barking dog, it never seems to solve the problem and just adds to the overall noise and stress of the whole thing.)

I managed to block her off and pointed towards the house. "Inside. Now."

She was headed there when another loud boom erupted from next door. She turned to charge towards the offending noise and I had to hop-skip my way into her path and get her turned back around and headed for the house again. "Inside. Go."

She went, bursting through the doggie door at the back of the house with enough force it was a miracle she didn't take the door with her.

I turned towards the six-foot wooden fence, ready to give Lucas Dean a piece of my mind, but before I could reach it, Fancy came charging around from the front of the house and resumed her barking.

(That was a rather unfortunate feature of our new home. It had doggie doors in the front **and** the back and unless I managed things properly Fancy would go in through one door but then immediately go right back out the other. She is too smart for my good, let me tell ya.)

By the time I wrangled Fancy back inside and blocked both doors so she'd stay there, things next door were once again quiet.

Who does that? Who sets off one or two loud explosions randomly during the middle of the day and then just goes on about their business as if it's nothing?

Is that fun? Can you even see fireworks in the middle of the day? I mean, really?

It seemed to me that the only reason someone would set off fireworks in the middle of the day is because they were a you-know-what who wanted to upset their neighbors.

I stewed about it all afternoon until Matt came home.

It was so nice to have my tall, dark, and handsome husband walk through our door and give me a kiss, his blue eyes shining with love.

(In theory. Turns out that after a long shift in a cop car he could've maybe used a shower first thing. Still, a little man-stink was worth overlooking for the fact that I, Maggie May Carver, was now married to Matthew Barnes and that we could finally be together in the same house.)

"Hey, Maggie. How was your day?" he asked.

Since my days pretty much consisted of playing Sudoku on the computer and reading in the backyard, I normally didn't have much to tell him. But that day...

"You need to talk to Lucas Dean. Immediately."

"Why? Is it the shorts? Because I'm happy to talk to him about the shorts."

I laughed. "No. It's not about the shorts."

"Are you sure? I'd be happy to cite him for some sort of indecency violation so he'd cover up better."

"I'm sure you would. And if you want to mention it to him while you're over there, I'd be more than happy to be spared that sight on a regular basis. The only man I want to see in shorts that short is you. And even then...Not really my thing."

He narrowed his eyes at me. "You can't pretend he doesn't look good half-naked."

"Oh, he does. But I see a man's soul not his six-pack abs and that man is ug-ly."

Matt laughed. "So what do you want me to talk to him about?"

I stepped back and paced the room, my hands clenched into fists. "Fireworks. He set off two today. And three yesterday. And two the day before that. It has to stop."

"Maggie. It's the week before the Fourth of July. That's going to happen."

"It's a fire hazard." I flicked my blonde braid behind my shoulder and crossed my arms, glaring him down.

He raised an eyebrow at me.

"It is. And it upsets Fancy. Plus think about all the little kids and babies down for naps that were probably woken up by that. Or the veterans with PTSD. Or the...raccoons. And skunks. He keeps this up someday someone is going to get sprayed by a startled skunk."

Matt pressed his lips together. I knew he was trying not to laugh at me. "You're worried about the skunks, huh?"

"I'm serious about this, Matt. You talk to him or I will. And we both know that when I talk to people I make unfortunate death threats."

He squeezed my upper arms and smiled. "But you don't mean them."

I paused. "In this case I might."

"Maggie...I may be your husband, but I'm also still an officer of the law. Maybe don't joke about killing people in front of me?"

"Even if they deserve it?"

"**Especially** if they deserve it. Makes it much more likely they'll actually get killed and I'll have to investigate you."

I rolled my eyes. "Please. Like anyone would kill Luke. The universe is not that kind." I took Matt's hands in mine and gave him my best doe-eyed look. "So you'll talk to him for me?"

"Can it wait until after dinner?"

I nodded and wrinkled my nose. "Actually, dinner and a shower." I sniffed again. "Shower first."

I gave him a quick kiss on the cheek to take the sting out of my words and then headed into the kitchen to check on the pub-style cod I had baking away in the oven.

A Fouled-Up Fourth

(My latest round of panic-buying of meat I'd decided to diversify a bit and was now stuck with various weird fish dishes that weren't bad, but weren't as emotionally satisfying as a good red-blooded steak. Life, I tell ya. If it isn't one thing it's another.)

CHAPTER 2

The next day Luke was outside mowing his yard when Fancy and I stepped out our front door.

Unfortunately, our front yard did not have a six-foot fence so I had to actually see him. (It had a cute little white picket fence instead, which was theoretically what you want in the perfect home, except, well, neighbors.)

I paused for a moment to smile at him because he was actually wearing a tank top with his too-short shorts.

He stopped the mower and sauntered over, pulling his baseball cap down a little lower. **He** was a good-looking man. On the surface. If you go for that "let's sneak off behind the bleachers for some fun" look.

He leaned forward, pressing his hands into the gaps between the white slats on the fence as I kept Fancy from going over to say hi. "Didn't figure you for a snitch, Sunshine," he said.

"I hate that word, you know. Snitch. It's the type of word people who do bad things use to make other people feel guilty about telling on them."

He winked. "I think that would be the point, don't you? Why'd you call the cops on me, Maggie?"

"I didn't call the cops on you." I fought the urge to cross my arms defensively. I hadn't called the cops. I'd waited until Matt got home.

"No? Then why was Matt on my doorstep first thing this morning, dressed in his full uniform with his hand on his gun, wanting to talk to me for just a moment?"

I tried not to laugh at the image. "Seems he doesn't like you peacocking around." I nodded at the tank top. "Nice to see you wearing some real clothes for once."

He leaned forward. "Like I told him. It's not my fault his wife can't take her eyes off me." He dropped his voice lower and purred, "You know, you ever get lonely over there, I'm right next door. I'm sure I could satisfy your needs..."

I said something back that I won't repeat here. I'm sure you can figure it out.

He just laughed and took a half-step back. "Always such a pleasure to talk to you, Maggie. By the way, you should know I've still got a **whole** lot of fireworks that need setting off and I plan to do so."

"I thought Matt talked to you about that."

"He did. Told me I couldn't set them off except for the weekend. So Friday night? Get ready to rumble."

Before I could say anything else about it, he turned and strolled away, adding an extra little swagger to his step just for my benefit. I huffed and stormed over to my grandpa's where I'd been headed before Luke accosted me, poor Fancy trailing along at my side trying to figure out what was wrong.

After I politely waited for my grandpa to open the door and let me inside, I stomped into the kitchen and grabbed a Coke. "I hate that man. I hate him with a passion. I wish he'd die."

Fancy fled for the backyard as my grandpa leaned against the doorway into the kitchen, looking as calm and composed as ever in his blue jeans and short-sleeved checkered button-up shirt. He was eighty-three, but you'd never know it from looking at him. He could easily pass for a man in his sixties since his hair was a faded brown instead of gray and he'd kept trim.

"Who is it you want to die today?" he asked, nonplussed.

"Who do you think? Lucas Dean. Haven't you heard the fireworks he keeps setting off?" I barely stopped myself from slamming the fridge closed, knowing that my grandpa would have my head if I did.

"You're upset about fireworks?" He raised one eyebrow.

"Do you realize how much they upset Fancy? It's horrible. It's **torture**. And anyone who tortures my dog deserves to die." I threw myself onto one of the kitchen table chairs.

"Maggie May."

"What?" I snapped, taking a long, long sip of soda. "You know hurting animals is the first step to becoming a serial killer."

He shook his head and grabbed himself a Coke, but much more calmly. "Fireworks are as American as apple pie and the flag," he said, joining me at the table.

"Oh please. I hate the Fourth of July. All it is is a holiday where people get drunk and show how American they are by setting off loud explosives that traumatize small animals and half their neighbors. It's absurd. Whatever its original purpose, it doesn't serve it anymore. Not that any of them do, really. Name me one holiday that isn't about getting drunk or getting gifts."

He raised an eyebrow at me, but didn't comment further.

I looked closer. "You're not planning on setting off fireworks, too, are you?"

"Here? No. Maybe down at the park. But that's far enough away you shouldn't be too upset by them."

I nodded, still wanting to punch something. (Not that I've ever punched anything in my life. That would hurt. It's just the thought of punching something that gives me a deep feeling of satisfaction sometimes. Call it positive visualization. Almost as good as the real thing and far less likely to land me in jail.)

"So." I took a deep breath, calming myself and deciding it was time to change the subject. "Lesley coming over for lunch?"

He nodded. "Would you like to join us?"

"If you don't mind. All I'm going to do if I stay home is storm around the house thinking of creative ways to kill Lucas Dean. And my cop husband has informed me that's not something I should do. Especially if I then talk about it out loud."

My grandpa smiled. "He does have a point."

"Yeah, whatever. How's the baseball season going?"

It wasn't the most eloquent way to change the subject, but I knew my grandpa and he loved coaching the local baseball team. We weren't a big town—Creek had about forty houses total—but every year we somehow managed to gather together enough kids to form a local baseball team that my grandpa coached. It was the highlight of his year working with those kids and I was so glad he was going to be able to coach them this year in safety.

"We have some great players this year..." he said as we sat down at the kitchen table.

We spent the next twenty minutes talking about batting averages and which kids had the heart to persevere even if they weren't there yet.

It was good. Good to spend time with my grandpa talking about something that mattered to him and just relaxing and enjoying the day.

I'd almost forgotten about Lucas Dean, but then...BOOM. Another firework went off. I cussed up a storm as I headed out the front door to tell him exactly what I thought of him, leaving my poor grandpa to calm down Fancy.

CHAPTER 3

Luke was standing in his front yard, grinning like an idiot, as I rushed towards him.

"It wasn't me," he said, holding his hands up in the air.

I jabbed my finger at him. "Then who was it? Because it sounded like it came from here."

"You gonna call the cops on me, Maggie. Take that husband of yours away from writing speeding tickets to give me another lecture about the rights of **dogs**?"

"I hate you. You know that?"

"Now, now, Maggie. Don't get so worked up. You're such a buzzkill."

I barely stopped myself from stomping my foot. "Another one of those words that people love to throw around when they're being jerks and don't want someone to stop their fun."

A man I didn't recognize came banging out of Luke's house. He was about the same age as us—late 30's—but hadn't kept himself in very good shape. His white t-shirt was stained in a few spots and untucked where it hung over his belly which in turn hung over his loose-fitting jeans. He had a nasty glint in his eye.

"Who's this?" he asked, eyeing me up and down in a way that made my blood boil.

I opened my mouth to tell him none of his business, but Luke beat me to it. "My neighbor. The one I told you wasn't going to appreciate you setting off that firework."

The guy scratched the sparse patch of stubble on his chin. "Huh. She gonna be around when you have your party on Friday?"

"Probably. She's always around killing my fun." Luke winked at me.

"Too bad." He turned back towards the house. "Come help me with the keg when you're done flirtin'. I'd like to tap it and see if it's any good since we're confined to this local brew stuff what with the valley being shut down and all."

I grimaced in disgust at the thought that I was **flirting** with Luke. This was not some rom-com enemies-to-lovers story. I was married, for one. And Luke was an ass, for two. (Yes, I did just use that word.) Plus, any man who'd do something to upset my dog was an absolute no. That is not redeemable in my opinion.

"Better get going," Luke said. "See you around, Sunshine." He turned and swaggered back inside.

That left me standing in the middle of the street fuming at his front door with nowhere to direct my anger. Fortunately for me, Lesley pulled into my grandpa's driveway just then and I immediately calmed down. She's so mellow and put together it's almost impossible to stay angry when she's around.

She stepped out of her perfectly maintained Lincoln and waved my way. "Hi, Maggie."

I walked over to her. "Hi, Lesley. How are you?"

Even on a random afternoon when all she was doing was going over to see my grandpa (who was her husband, but they still weren't living together), she looked perfectly put together, her pure-white hair styled into a subtle chignon, her jewelry that perfect balance of noticeable but not gauche. She was even wearing makeup and short high heels to go with her tailored slacks.

I adored her. She was great for my grandpa. But I was glad that the world didn't expect that level of put-togetherness from me, because I would've never managed to pull it off. It didn't matter how much time and care I put into getting dolled up, there was always something wrong with my outfit. A run in my hose. A chipped nail. A loose string on my hem. I'd never managed perfection a single day in my life.

Which was fine with me. Because perfection was simply not something I strove for. Too much effort for too little gain. I was pretty sure when I went to my grave no one was going to stand around and talk about how unfortunate it was that my shirts were sometimes wrinkled.

(And if they did, well, that was on them not me.)

"Are you joining us for lunch?" she asked.

"If that's okay with you." I silently pleaded with my eyes that she'd say yes.

"Of course, dear. Will you grab the casserole from the backseat?"

"Absolutely."

As we walked inside I sniffed at the edge of the aluminum foil to see what she'd made. Whatever it was, it smelled remarkably delicious. All fatty cheese and meat and bread of some sort. My stomach grumbled in anticipation.

My grandpa held the door open for us. "I gave that mutt of yours an ice cream to calm her down," he grumbled at me after giving Lesley a kiss on the cheek.

"She's not a mutt, Grandpa. And don't act like you don't love her just as much as I do." I handed him the casserole. "I'll go check on her, make sure she's okay. By the way, this time it wasn't Luke, it was some guy who's helping him set up for a big party on Friday night."

"What happened?" Lesley asked as I went in search of Fancy.

I heard my grandpa start to fill her in as I stepped outside. Fancy looked up at me, but didn't stop licking at her ice cream for a single moment. Once she got started on those things she was relentless. Other dogs I knew just took the entire container in their mouths and crunched it to pieces, paper wrapper and all. But Fancy would sit there for five minutes straight licking at the ice cream over and over again until it was all gone, leaving the container behind in almost pristine condition.

It was like that old Tootsie Pop commercial where they asked how many licks does it take to get to the center of the Tootsie Pop. Fancy would know the answer. Most dogs would just bite the thing before the end like the owl, but not Fancy

What can I say? My dog is as weird as I am.

I patted her head. "You okay, girl?"

She just kept licking.

"I'll take that as a yes."

I glanced in the direction of Luke's house. Clearly I was going to have to do something on Friday, because I could not have fireworks going off right next door for hours without it completely traumatizing Fancy. I growled in annoyance. Why couldn't he just go to the rodeo to see fireworks like everyone else?

CHAPTER 4

Fortunately, Jamie, my best friend, and Mason, her somewhat-acceptable-when-he-wasn't-being-too-obnoxiously-rich husband, invited me over for a little pre-Fourth barbecue on Friday night. Which meant that I was able to take Fancy and get away from the house before Luke's party got into full swing.

It had started around two with a bunch of uncouth men hanging out in his front yard getting drunk, but at least they'd held off on the fireworks until after I left.

Jamie, being the agreeable, wonderful person she is had told me I could come by at any time I wanted, but I didn't head over there until four.

She and Mason lived on a large plot of land outside town in a very colossal mountain-man-chic sort of home that involved lots of wood and natural stone. (It was his before they got married. If Jamie'd had a say there would have been more...**grace** to the place. More subtlety. But it was what it was. I had no doubt that given a few years she'd tone down what could be toned down.)

She was standing on the porch when I pulled up, glowing with happiness. And I do mean glowing. You know how they say some people get that pregnancy glow? Well, that was Jamie. About five months in she had the cutest baby bump in the world and was all health and joy from head to toe. Honestly, I don't think she'd stopped smiling since she found out she was pregnant.

She had her long brown hair braided back from her face and was wearing a bright yellow sundress that made her the poster child for being happily pregnant. I could just see the words shining in the air over her head. "Pregnancy is great! You should be pregnant, too! Everyone should be!"

It wasn't fooling me though. **I** knew that pregnancy was not all cute little feet pushing against bellies and good hormone surges. I'd **heard** things. Maybe she just wasn't at that stage yet. Although, Jamie being Jamie, she'd probably just laugh and smile right on through to the end, swollen ankles, acid reflux, hemorrhoids, and all.

Although, if we're being honest here, it was the thought of not being allowed unlimited quantities of Coke that scared me the most when it came to being pregnant. Going through one of the most life-changing events you can experience without caffeine as a crutch?

Haha. No.

As soon as I let Fancy off her leash she went tearing around the side of the house to find Lulu. No longer a puppy, Lulu—Jamie's golden retriever—could now give Fancy a run for her money. Of course, she was still only about half Fancy's size. Fancy was a hundred-and-forty pounds, Lulu was probably seventy. But what Lulu had that Fancy didn't was stamina.

Within five minutes, Fancy was
ready to sprawl in the shade
somewhere and take a nap while Lulu
was still puppy pouncing around her
and yapping to keep going. Jamie
had never been the best at
disciplining Lulu, but fortunately
Mason had no problem being firm
with her, so we left him on guard
duty as Jamie excitedly led me
through the house to the baby's
room.

"I can't wait to show you what
we're going to do," she exclaimed as
we climbed up to the second floor
and made our way down the long
hallway towards the master bedroom.
She stopped at the room next door to
the master and opened it.

And...

Well, it was a room. Plain white
walls. Boring light gray carpet. At
least it didn't have the wood and
stone theme that dominated most of
the house. There was one small side
table by the door but nothing else.

Jamie stepped into the center of
the room. "So this is the room we're
going to use for the nursery. I finally
got all of Mason's stuff cleared out so

we can start painting and putting down the new carpet. Here."

She grabbed a binder off the table and shoved it into my hands. (Jamie loves binders. I was surprised there was only one so far.) She opened it up for me. "The first tab is the furniture we're going to order. What do you think?"

It was…fine. Nice white wood furniture. Nothing too exciting except the price tag. There was a rocking chair and a crib and a dresser and it all looked okay enough to me, but what did I know? I couldn't see from the picture what made the furniture better than a dresser you could get at Target. I'm sure it was much nicer. Probably last a hundred years or something. Too bad it was only needed for probably six months.

Fortunately, Jamie didn't really want my opinion, because she kept right on talking. "And the next tab is the paint colors we're going to use. It's so important these days to be gender-neutral, you know. So no trucks if it's a boy and no curly-haired dolls if it's a girl. Just puzzle toys and stuffed bears and things like that. We don't want to program our kids with unhealthy ideas."

"But what if your kid really loves trucks? Or curly-haired dolls? Are you just going to deny them?"

She blinked at me, like the thought had never occurred to her. "We're not going to allow them screen time."

"Still. I'm not even saying if you have a boy that he'll be the one who likes trucks. You could have a girl who likes trucks. Or action figures. Or building things. Or a boy who likes curly-haired dolls. You never know. But I'm pretty sure whatever gender your child is they're going to like some sort of gendered toy at some point."

She frowned, and I laughed and patted her on the shoulder. "Don't worry too much about it, Jamie. As it turns out, most kids grow up just fine no matter what their parents subject them to. So. Gender-neutral paint colors. And," I flipped to the next tab, "giraffes and teddy bears."

She nodded, but her brow was all wrinkly and she was pressing her lips together a little too tightly. As I watched in horror, her eyes filled with tears.

"What is it? What's wrong? Did I say something to upset you? Jamie!"

She shook her head. "It's nothing. I just..." She waved her hands around. "I want it to be perfect. I want to give this baby the best life they can possibly have. And there are so many decisions and so many ways it can go wrong and...Maggie, what do I do?"

I laughed and gave her a quick hug. "It'll be okay, Jamie. I think kids are pretty resilient, all things considered. And I've never seen you mess anything up in your entire life." I pushed back and looked her in the eye. "But even if you do mess this up a little bit, it's okay. You have Mason and you have me and you have all your other friends and you aren't alone in this. People have kids every day. Some of them probably barely crack a book about it before they're suddenly holding a screaming infant in their arms. They make it through. So you will, too. It's biology."

"But there are so many theories out there and so much you need to do.

And you have to feed them the right foods. And..."

"Jamie. Look at me. My mom put Karo syrup in water and fed it to me when I was a baby because I was so damned hungry all the time. But you know what? I turned out fine. Maybe with a certain soda addiction I wouldn't have had otherwise, but seriously. If our parents could do things like that—because you know your mother did crazy stuff like that, too—and we could turn out just fine, you'll be fine, too. Plus, honestly, a little bit of dirt and bad food and scraped knees is good for a kid. You can't coddle them too much if you actually want them to move on and be independent someday."

"Your mom gave you Karo syrup?"

I nodded. "**And** she let me run around pretty much buck naked until I was maybe three or four. I mean, not always, but there are definitely pictures enough to show it."

(My favorite one was of me sitting on the sink with a toothbrush in my mouth, tanned from head to toe so I'd obviously been spending a large amount of time outside sans clothes.

And, come to think of it, I was quite possibly even older than four in that photo. If I and the world could survive that, Jamie's kid was going to be just fine.)

Jamie bit her lip.

"It's going to be fine, Jamie. I know it will. You think maybe this was a bit of pregnancy hormones? I mean, I'm never a fan of when men suggest hormones as a cause for things, but I hear it's pretty real when it comes to pregnancy."

She chuckled. "Yeah, probably. Mason doesn't know what to do with me these days because half the time I'm happy and excited and half the time I'm scared and crying. Or angry. I **yelled** at him yesterday. I never yell. But he left a pan on the stove after he made breakfast. And it was filthy. Who does that?"

"Have you ever been to my home?"

She shuddered. "Yes."

I laughed and put an arm around her shoulders as I led her back down the hallway. "Try to give him a break, this is all new to him, too, you know."

She nodded. "I know. You're right. But it was filthy, Maggie. Just thinking about it now...Ugh."

As we walked down the stairs back to the main level Fancy scrambled to her feet from where she'd been lying at the base of the stairs.

"You silly goof," I told her, bending down to rub her ears and kiss her nose.

"Why didn't she just come up?" Jamie asked.

"Yeah, no. Fancy and stairs do not go together. That's one of the reasons I don't think we'll stay where we are long-term. Half of the square footage is up a flight of stairs Fancy won't use."

Mason came in from the back porch with a plateful of grilled hamburger patties that smelled delicious. "You'd actually choose your house to accommodate your dog?" he asked.

"Yes. Of course. Wouldn't you?"

He chuckled. "No."

"You and my grandpa. But for me Fancy's comfort is probably number two on the list of what I need in a home. My own comfort being number one."

"And Matt's comfort?" he asked.

"Matt's comfort is my comfort." I batted my eyes at him and made my way to the fridge to grab a Coke. Just the thought of being deprived of my beloved addiction made me need one.

As I watched Jamie and Mason set out all the fixings for cheeseburgers and banter back and forth, I couldn't help but smile. I was so happy for them and so glad to be able to just hang out with them and enjoy a good meal together.

We were all blessed. Truly.

CHAPTER 5

I stayed at their house until the sun went down and then gave it another hour just to be safe. I figured Luke couldn't possibly have more than an hour's worth of fireworks to set off.

I was wrong.

As I drove up the street towards my house I could see the haze from all the fireworks that had already been set off. Another one screamed its way into the sky as I reached my driveway, a group of men and women with beers gathered on the front lawn cheering as it exploded in a shower of bright lights.

"Welp. I guess we're going for a drive, Fancy," I said, continuing on past my house and turning back towards the highway.

The good thing about living in a fairly rural area is that I could easily find a stretch of road far enough from any homes that we could avoid more fireworks.

I drove along the highway towards Masonville with the windows down. It was a gorgeous night, the sky clear of clouds and a deep dark blue, the stars shining bright above us, the breeze that blew through my hair pleasantly cool but not cold.

I didn't even bother trying to go the speed limit. (For once.) I wasn't trying to get anywhere. I was just killing time. So I drove along slowly, enjoying the feel of the breeze and the sound of Lizz Wright crooning about how she idolized someone.

There's a peace to being away from everyone, driving down a two-lane road through the countryside when it's already dark out, your headlights and the stars the only light, the air carrying the scent of fresh, healthy vegetation and maybe a hint of rain.

By the time I turned around outside Masonville and headed back towards Creek I was actually feeling calm and happy. Let Luke and his friends

Aleksa Baxter

celebrate the holiday with too much
booze and bad decisions. I had what
I wanted: Fancy snoring away in the
back of the van, a gorgeous night,
and a gorgeous husband who'd be
home sometime around three or four
in the morning.

Of course, that peace evaporated
as soon as I returned home and saw
that Luke was **still** not done. Rather
than drive around even more and risk
some stupid drunk driver taking us
out, I decided I'd just barricade
Fancy and myself as far from the
noise as we could get and hope it
would be over soon.

I pulled into the driveway and
made my way around to Fancy's door.
I figured Luke would have the
courtesy to maybe refrain from
setting off the next firework until we
were inside. But no. Of course he
didn't.

(I should've known. Assholes gonna
asshole. But I always have this small
hope that my fellow humans are
actually going to prove to be decent
even though I should know better by
now.)

As I let Fancy out of the van, a Roman candle went off ten feet away shooting loud streaking light and sparks in every direction. Poor Fancy lost it and started barking her head off, lunging towards the noise and light.

Luke just laughed.

I shouted four words at him. I'm sure you can guess which ones.

Because, seriously? Who does that? I know you're not supposed to cuss at a neighbor, but why can't neighbors return the same respect? I mean, really? You set one of those things off when there's a dog right there?

Yeah. Bleep you, Lucas Dean.

I herded Fancy inside as Luke continued to laugh at us. But I stopped in the door and turned and looked at him with every ounce of hate I felt. Seriously, some people can die as far as I'm concerned and the world would be a better place for it.

(Yeah, I know, how awful of me. What can I say? I'm pretty sure I must be one of those people who'd actually kill the enemy during war, not just shoot around them like most soldiers who haven't been trained supposedly do.)

Fancy and I spent the next half hour huddled on the floor of the walk-in closet in the bedroom with all the bedroom windows blocked with heavy blankets to muffle the sound as much as possible.

Even with all of my effort, Fancy still occasionally barked. I swear, a few of the ones they set off actually shook the house. But eventually they tapered off to just the occasional small pop of sound here or there and we were able to fall asleep on the floor, side-by-side.

When Matt finally came home from work at three or four or whatever time it was, Fancy immediately jumped to her feet and cried until I woke up and let her out.

"There you are," Matt laughed as we emerged from the closet. "You okay?"

"I'd be better if Lucas Dean were dead," I said as I walked Fancy to the kitchen and opened the back door for her, figuring it was safe enough to let her outside now. If someone still had fireworks to set off I'd send Matt after them.

"Maggie, what did I say about making death threats against people?"

"Not a good idea. Blah, blah, blah. Yeah, yeah, yeah." I leaned into his chest, still half asleep.

Matt pulled back and kissed the tip of my nose. "It's not, you know."

I snuggled back against him and sighed in contentment. "I know. But you can't expect me to control my thoughts when I'm this tired, can you?"

"Fair enough. Come on. Let's get you into a real bed. The floor doesn't look all that comfortable."

"It's not. Trust me." (The carpet in that closet was **old**. And thin. And my hip and shoulder hurt from lying on what was essentially bare ground.)

We shuffled down the hall, linked together in that casual way couples have, and I couldn't help but smile. I'd never actually pictured myself in a

Aleksa Baxter

moment like that, but now that I was in it, I couldn't imagine a better place to be.

Aleksa Baxter

moment like that, but now that I was in it, I couldn't imagine a better place to be.

CHAPTER 6

Fancy woke me the next morning at 5:37 AM on the dot with a small little cry that said it was time to rejoin the world of the living. Rain, shine, summer, winter, it doesn't matter to Fancy. Too early for sanity is the time to be awake.

Since it was getting towards the middle of summer, I leashed her up and took her for her walk first thing before it could get warm. I muttered a few extra curses at Luke as we walked by his house and I saw all the burned-out, discarded firework wrappers spread all over the street. Not only had he set off fireworks for hours, he was a litter bug, too.

Figured.

But I couldn't hold on to my grumpiness for too long. It was a gorgeous, gorgeous morning with enough clouds in the sky over the mountains to paint them in sherbet pinks and oranges. And no one else was up, so there was this expectant stillness to the day. Like anything was possible.

Fancy and I made our way down to the baseball park and sprawled in the grass in center field. She was in her happy place because she liked to be outside in really nice grass. I was, too, because I loved the view of Creek in the early morning with its little homes and the mountains surrounding me on all sides and the blue, blue sky above.

It was glorious. Amazing. Perfect.

Which is why you know it didn't last. Not even long enough for me to walk back home.

A truck screeched to a halt at the edge of the ball field. "That's not good," I muttered as I narrowed my eyes trying to figure out who it was. "Oh, yeah. Definitely not good."

It was Trish, my sister-in-law? (I was still getting used to all the family relationships I'd married into.) She was red-haired, long-legged, and always in some sort of trouble or other.

She had the worst taste in men I'd ever seen. And I say that even though she'd finally settled down and married Matt's brother, Jack. When she stayed with me during the early parts of the lockdown she'd spent far more time than I thought was advisable talking to Luke through the front fence. And Jack, as good as he was with Trish's son, Sam, was about one step away from turning back to his criminal roots on any given day.

So Trish seeing me at the ball field and deciding to come talk to me at six in the morning was a very, very bad sign.

"Hey, Trish," I called as she made her way towards me in her slim-fitted jeans and a tank top.

Fancy wagged her tail once, but didn't make a move to get up. (She loves pretty much any man, but women she's mostly indifferent to.)

"Hey, Maggie," Trish said when she finally came close enough to not have to shout. She tried to smile, but it was forced.

This was definitely not good. I wanted to close my eyes and lie back in the grass and pretend she wasn't standing there, but that's not what family does, is it? Or polite people, but I'm not one of those.

"What's up?" I asked.

"Um..." She twirled a lock of hair around her finger and chewed on her lip like she was still a teenager.

"Sit. Seriously. You're looming over me up there." Maybe sitting would calm her down enough for her to tell me what was going on.

She glanced at the grass like it would permanently ruin her jeans, but finally sat down across from me. I realized as I looked at her that even that early in the morning she was wearing mascara and lipstick and had clearly taken the time to style her hair not just throw it back like I always do.

"What is it, Trish? Is it Jack? Is it Sam? What are you doing out so early?"

"No, it's not Jack or Sam." She fiddled with her perfectly-manicured nails, not willing to look at me.

"Well then?" I asked, losing patience.

She bit her thumb for a moment before answering. "I was just at Luke's."

"Luke's? Lucas Dean's? My neighbor's?"

She nodded.

I tried not to roll my eyes. "I didn't see you when I left the house. So you either weren't there that long or you'd parked your truck out of view somewhere. Which is it?"

"I...I wasn't there very long."

"So....? What happened? Why are we having this conversation?" I knew she was family now, but c'mon already. Tell me what the problem was.

She fiddled with her nails some more, not looking at me.

"Trish," I snapped, wanting to shake her until she just said whatever it was she wanted to tell me.

"He's dead. Luke's...dead." She curled in on herself like a pretzel, twisting her legs up and wrapping her arms around them.

I sighed in disgust. "Of course he is."

Because that would be my luck, wouldn't it? Most people go through their life and they never know anyone who gets killed or dies unexpectedly. But me? Since moving to the Baker Valley? Well, let's just say the body count was not encouraging. And it would have to be Luke who was dead, the man I'd not so subtly threatened with significant bodily harm and who lived right next door.

My life. I tell ya.

Trish stared at me. "You knew already?"

"No. I did not know already. Just...Ignore me. Sometimes I say what I'm thinking and I really shouldn't." I pinched the bridge of my nose. "So Luke's dead."

She nodded.

"Was it natural causes? Did he slip and fall while drunk?"

One could always hope. Although since Trish was talking to me about it in the middle of a ballpark, it wasn't likely.

"Not unless he slipped and fell on a knife. In his back."

I rubbed at my face, trying to think. It was too early for this. Just because I could get up at unholy hours, didn't mean my mind was awake yet. "Did you touch anything while you were there?" I asked.

She nodded.

"**What** did you touch?"

"Um…" Trish looked up at the sky, trying to remember and ticking each item off on her fingers as she named them. "The rock where he keeps his spare key. The key. The front door. The table by the front door. The door knob—both sides. The kitchen table. A beer bottle. Um…"

"Stop. That's enough." I sighed. "Did you touch the body? Step in the blood? Move it around any?"

"The blood? Did I move the blood?" she asked, confused.

"The body. Did you move the body?"

"Um...I don't think so. He wasn't wearing a shirt and he was facedown so I could see the wound without moving him. And it was pretty clear he was dead, so I didn't feel for a pulse or anything." She glanced at the bottom of her sandals. "No blood."

"Right. So as far as the cops or anyone else knows, you could've left those prints there some other time."

She nodded.

"Why didn't you just call the cops when you found him?" (Instead of ruining my delightful morning in the park, I wanted to add.)

"Because it looks bad. I mean...I'm married to Jack and..."

"Yeah. It does." I gave her a look. That look you give a woman who makes terrible choices in men who's just told you she was trying to visit some guy who wasn't her husband at six in the morning.

She shrunk away from me. "Jack's a good guy. I love him. I do. And he's great with Sam. But with everything that's been going on he's been working really hard. He isn't there much. And Luke..."

"Was."

She nodded.

I wanted to say more, but her marriage issues were not my immediate problem. Not yet at least.

"What made you go by the house? Was this pre-arranged?" I asked, trying to figure out if I was sitting across from a murderer or not.

"No. It wasn't like that. We normally text back and forth in the middle of the night. Neither one of us sleeps too well." She started pulling up the grass and stacking it in a small pile, reminding me of that time when I was six and my neighbor hired me to pull grass for him so he could make little bags of Colorado Weed that he sealed with a roach clip and sold to tourists. Only many years later did I finally understand why my mom was so horrified when she found out about it.

Unaware of my wandering thoughts, she continued, "But I texted him at two and he didn't answer. And then I kept texting him

Aleksa Baxter

every half hour or so until six and he still didn't answer. So I figured I better go check on him."

"Why? For all you know he could've been with some floozy from the party."

"I know. But when I left the party he said to text him later. And there was really no one there that looked like his type."

I laughed. "Luke's type is anyone breathing between the ages of seventeen and seventy."

"He's not like that, Maggie. It's just an act."

I tried not to choke on that one.

"So what do we do?" she asked.

"Could just stay out of it," I suggested with a hopeful smile.

I wasn't a huge fan of calling the cops when I found dead bodies. It seldom worked out well. Then again, **not** calling the cops hadn't worked out so well for me either. Really, when you find a dead body it's kind of a lose-lose situation whatever you do.

She looked at me in shock. "He's dead. We have to tell someone."

I narrowed my eyes. Did we? Did we really? I mean, someone else was bound to drop by at some point, weren't they? And not like Trish had any interesting information about the murder.

Then again...I was pretty sure this fell under the heading of things you're supposed to tell your spouse about, especially when your spouse is a cop. Matt and I had agreed that everyone has little secrets they keep and that we didn't really need full unfettered access to one another's emails and social media accounts and all that, but we'd also agreed not to keep any big secrets from each other either.

I figured the fact that Matt's brother's wife had found a dead body probably fell under the big secret category. Especially since I had also threatened to kill the victim on more than one occasion, including just a few hours before Trish found him dead.

Darn it.

I sighed. This married thing, it made life a lot more complicated.

"Okay. Here's what we'll do. We'll tell Matt. See what he thinks about it and go from there. Just stay somewhere he can reach you."

She squeezed my arm. "Thanks, Maggie. I knew you'd know what to do."

I resisted the urge to snort at her comment. I had no clue what to do. But hopefully Matt would.

As Fancy and I trudged back home, I grumbled about how it was far too early in the morning to be dealing with murder. Far too early. Murders should only be committed or discovered after ten in the morning at the earliest. And ideally after noon. And before six. Why ruin a good evening?

But no. People had to be all inconvenient when they were murdered, didn't they?

CHAPTER 7

Matt, of course, was still in bed when I returned home. I couldn't blame him, he'd worked a late shift and was going to have to work another one that night.

I sat on the bed and looked at him for a long moment, sprawled on his belly, his mouth slightly open as he almost but not quite snored. I loved every line of him even if he wasn't as perfectly handsome this up-close as he'd been the day I met him. Reality does that, you know. Takes away all the shine. But good thing is it replaces it with something much deeper and more lasting.

I debated not waking him and just telling him about Luke when he finally did get up which would probably be in about four hours or so. That was fair, wasn't it? He wouldn't feel betrayed by that would he? I'd still be telling him about what Trish had found at the first opportunity I had. I'd just also be giving someone else a chance to discover the body first.

Unfortunately, he's a light sleeper. All that military training, I suspect. He opened one eye and looked at me. "Hey. How was your walk? Come back for a cuddle?" He rolled over and lifted his arm up, inviting me to burrow in against his chest.

"I wish. Unfortunately..."

He yawned and flipped over onto his back, tucking one hand behind his head. "Unfortunately?"

I stared at the ceiling so I wouldn't have to see his expression as I asked, "Remember how I'm not supposed to wish people dead because they might end up dead and then it would be all awkward?"

"Yes." He was fully awake now.

"Well..."

"Lucas Dean is dead?"

I nodded.

He sat up. "And how do you know this?"

"That's the even more awkward part." I rubbed at the back of my neck as I filled him in on Trish's little visit and our conversation at the ball field.

By the time I was done he was already half-dressed and looking for his phone. "Any reason for Trish to lie about this?" he asked. "Do you think she could've done it?"

"No. And no reason to lie that I can think of. She doesn't strike me as the diabolically-clever, plant-an-alibi sort."

He sat back down on the bed. "It's going to kill Jack to find out about those text messages. And the fact that she came here looking for Luke."

"Does he have to know?" I asked, wincing as I said the words because I already knew the answer.

Matt gave me a long, long look.

I hunched my shoulders. "What? It's a fair question. He loves Sam so much and Luke's dead so not like anything is going to happen there with Trish, so why force him into making a choice maybe he doesn't want to have to make?"

"He needs to know, Maggie. Luke isn't the only one willing to pursue a woman he shouldn't."

"True. Up until a little bit ago, Jack was in that camp, too, you know."

He rubbed his fingers through his hair, ruffling it in five different directions. "Some people manage to work through these things. It doesn't have to be the end."

It was my turn to give him a long, long look. "It would be for me. Just sayin'."

"Oh me, too. Just so **you** know."

"Alright then. As long as we're agreed on that." I smiled at him.

He smiled back. "We are."

We sat there for another long, awkward moment until he finally stood. "Well, better go see what I can see."

I followed him to the kitchen. "You know, Luke did leave a lot of firework debris in the yard. Maybe you could knock on his door to tell him to pick it up?"

"And then go inside when he doesn't answer even though I'd normally just assume he was too hungover and swing back by later?"

I shrugged. "Could be something is visible from one of the windows."

He shook his head. "Or I could just tell dispatch I was tipped to the fact that there was a dead body in his house and do it the right way." He tweaked my nose. "You're a bad influence on me, Maggie."

"Clearly not bad enough." I nodded towards the phone in his hand. "I was just trying to keep Trish out of it."

"I know. But if she was sending him text messages all night, there's no way to keep her out. She'll be interviewed no matter what. Might as well be sooner rather than later."

"Good point."

I went to feed Fancy her breakfast while Matt called it in.

CHAPTER 8

By ten that morning there were three cop cars pulled up outside Lucas Dean's house. My grandpa came to join me in my yard as I stood and watched Matt talk to Sue, the coroner, while two other officers brought a body bag out.

"What happened?" my grandpa asked.

"What do you think?"

"Really? Someone killed Luke?"

I nodded. "Certainly no lack of suspects is there? I mean pretty much every father of a teenaged daughter and every husband in the county has to be at least considered for a moment."

"And every neighbor who threatened to kill him for setting off fireworks, especially after last night's display." He gave me a pointed look.

I glanced sideways at him. "That's not funny, Grandpa."

"No. But it's true. I told you it wasn't a good idea to walk around threatening to kill the man."

"Yeah, yeah. You and Matt."

"Who found him?" he asked.

I scrunched up my face, trying to decide what to say. It was going to get out anyway, wasn't it? Can't keep a secret like that in a small town. Still. It felt a little gossipy to be the one passing it on.

"Trish. She told me. I told Matt. He called it in."

My grandpa raised an eyebrow but didn't say any more about it.

"Don't tell anyone, though," I added. "I mean, it'll probably get out, but, you know."

"Alright. As long as you promise not to get involved in investigating the murder."

I laughed. "Please. Like I would. Whoever killed Lucas Dean did the world a favor."

"Maggie May." He used that tone of voice that said I'd done something wrong like forget to clean up the bathroom or wash the dishes.

"What? I am a firm believer that there are certain people who make the world a worse place than it needs to be. And that if those people were not around that the world would be, on balance, a nicer, kinder place to live. Lucas Dean was one of those people."

He shook his head in disappointment. "If you went around killing every philandering loud-mouth who liked fireworks you'd be taking out a large part of the population. Maybe save your divine wrath for actively evil people like Ted Little."

I shuddered at the name. "That man, too. Ugh. Thanks for the reminder, Grandpa."

He turned to look at me, searching my face. "But you can see the difference between the two, can't you, Maggie May?"

I looked back at him, holding his gaze. "Look, Grandpa, here's the deal. While I fully believe that there are people who make the world a worse place by being in it I'd never actually advocate for taking those people out. Even Ted Little. Because I'd have no control over who got to wield that sort of power. And, as you point out, my list of people who make the world worse could be very different from someone else's. That's how we get frickin' holy wars, right? You don't believe in the right divine power, so you must die? I get it. I do. But there's a little fantasy world in my head where I get to point to bad drivers and mean people and, poof, vanish them to some other alternate reality where they no longer make my life unpleasant. And in that little fantasy world, Lucas Dean would make my list of people who go poof."

I crossed my arms and turned back to see them closing the door to the coroner's van. I added, "He laughed when Fancy freaked out over the fireworks, Grandpa. Laughed. Not a single sign of remorse. And don't even get me started on how he treated Jamie all those years. Or Katie. Or any number of other women."

"Hm." My grandpa grunted as he stared forward, arms crossed.

"What?" I demanded, exhausted and annoyed.

"Nothing. Just keep in mind that people who think the way you do about setting certain people aside and aren't so hesitant to use their powers are how otherwise decent people end up spending years of their life in jail. Unless you think a man deserves to be in jail for life because he stole one little thing? Or sold a little pot?" He looked at me sideways, one eyebrow raised.

I sighed and rolled my eyes. "Alright, Jean Valjean, you've made your point. I'll now go sing Kumbaya and love and accept everyone, no matter how horrible they make my life."

"Maggie May," he snapped.

"Sorry," I snapped right back.

I was kind of sorry. I mean, he had a point. But...

I know. He had a point.

I mean, he was living proof that bad decisions when you're younger don't have to define who you become. And if he hadn't eventually been given a second chance think of all the kids he'd coached whose lives would've been less because of his absence. Kids like Matt.

And what about me. Until Matt, after I lost my parents my grandparents were all I had in this world. My grandpa was my anchor. If no one had given him that second chance—or third chance as it turns out—where would I be?

So, yeah, fine. Forgiveness. Blah, blah, blah. It's wonderful, it's great. We should all do it.

But I still wasn't going to shed a single tear for Lucas Dean. Or be sad about the fact that he was gone.

Jamie was, though, which is why I excused myself and drove on over there before the gossip mill could reach her. She was blissfully happy with Mason and so much better off with him than she'd ever been with Luke, but fact was that Luke had been "that guy" for most of her teen years and well into her twenties and thirties and you don't just forget that because you find something better.

CHAPTER 9

That night I fixed myself a big, old celebratory dinner of petite filet mignon wrapped in bacon, baked potato, and grilled asparagus. It was heavenly. And Matt wasn't there to make me feel bad about it. I luxuriated in a peaceful evening devoid of fireworks next door and filled with the delicious taste of high-quality red meat. I even had a glass of red wine to go with it.

(I know. I'm horrible. But we long ago established that fact.)

Luke being gone was like removing that little pebble that's been stuck in the toe of your boot all day rubbing your foot raw. It was such a relief. I just knew things were going to get better.

Except they didn't.

Because the unimaginative police could only see two suspects: Trish, because she'd found the body in the middle of the night, which, fair enough. And me. Seriously, just because I'd walked around telling people I wanted him dead did not mean I killed him. Didn't they realize I was smarter than that?

(If I was actually going to kill someone I certainly wouldn't tell everyone about it right before I did it. Come on now.)

And really, the people I had told about that should've kept their mouths shut. But one of the things I loved about Matt was that he was the guy who wouldn't shy away from doing the right thing even when it was a challenge. So the next afternoon I found myself once again in the Creek jail interview room sitting across from Officer Clark and my husband.

That room was not designed to make a person want a return visit. It was poorly lit, cramped, and smelled slightly of disinfectant and stale body odor. There might've also been the scent of various bodily fluids, but I stared straight ahead and tried really hard not to think about it.

"Maggie," Matt said, "where's your lawyer?"

"Do I need one? I mean, really? We both know I did not do this."

He crossed his arms and stared me down, his eyes begging me to take this seriously. Surprisingly enough, Officer Clark didn't step in and try to get me talking but instead waited for Matt and me to finish our silent conversation.

Finally, I rolled my eyes. "Fine. Give me a minute." I pulled my phone out of my purse and dialed Mason Maxwell's number.

"Ms. Carver. How can I help you?"

I glared at Matt because I couldn't glare through the phone at Mason. "You're married to my best friend, Mason, you can call me Maggie."

"Then this is a personal call?" he asked.

"No," I growled, thinking it was a very good thing he wasn't there in the room with me the way he was being so obnoxious.

"Let me guess. The police want to talk to you about Lucas Dean's murder and you want me present while they question you."

"Pretty much."

"When?"

"We're sitting in the interrogation room right now if you wouldn't mind dropping by."

I could hear him sigh through the phone and pictured him pinching the bridge of his nose, reminding himself how much he loved his wife. "Tell me you have a better alibi for this murder than you did for the last one."

"I can promise you no one saw me running away from the crime scene this time around. Beyond that...Well, maybe not so much." (Matt had been at work when Luke was killed after all.)

"Is that because you weren't there? Or because you **walked** away?" he asked, all snide and annoying.

"Mason Maxwell," I snapped, fed up with his stupid questions. I was not in the mood to be poked at by an uptight jerk whose only redeeming quality was that he'd somehow convinced my best friend to marry him and bear his spawn.

(Yes, I know. I was being unfair. He's actually a decent enough guy once you get to know him, but did he have to be so **lawyerly**?)

"It is a fair question, Ms. Carver," he replied, completely calm.

I took a deep breath before answering. "I wasn't there. Now, can you please get down here so we can clear this matter up? I had to leave Fancy with my grandpa and she's going to have a sick tummy by the time I get out of here because he feeds her a treat every time she bats her eyes at him."

There was a slight pause. "You realize I do have other clients."

"I do. But I also know that you probably have orders from Jamie to drop everything and come help me out as soon as I call. Am I right?"

He sighed. "You are. I'll be there in ten minutes."

I hung up and smiled at Matt and Officer Clark. "My attorney will be here in ten. Any chance I can run home and grab a Coke while we're waiting?"

"No," Officer Clark answered. "You're a suspect here for questioning in a murder. You can't just leave."

Before I could open my mouth to respond, Matt put a hand on his shoulder. "It's alright. I'll escort her home, Ben. She won't be out of my sight for a moment."

As Matt and I stepped outside into the almost too-hot late afternoon heat, I shook my head. "That man needs therapy, Matt."

"Who?"

"Officer Clark. Honestly, what is wrong with him? He wasn't going to let me go home to grab a Coke? Some people take their jobs way too seriously."

"That's because there are protocols, Maggie. And those protocols do not involve letting a suspect leave the premises to obtain a personal beverage and bring it back into the interview room."

"Not like I'm grabbing myself a beer."

"Maggie." He grabbed my upper arms and leaned down so we were eye-to-eye. "You need to take this seriously. You are a suspect in a murder of a man you were known not to like. You have no alibi for the time of the murder. I know you think it's something you can just laugh off because you obviously didn't do it, but the more you do that the more seriously we have to treat it. Don't make me arrest my own wife. Especially if it's just because she wants to be difficult."

I ran my tongue along the bottom of my top teeth as I stared back at him. Finally, I sighed. "Fine. I will be the model interview witness so we can get this behind us."

"Thank you," Matt said in that tone of voice that implied he should've never had to ask me to behave in the first place.

CHAPTER 10

We walked the rest of the way home and back in silence, but I was a model witness for the entire hour and thirty minutes of questioning.

How they came up with that many questions when I hadn't done anything, I don't know. But they walked me through my entire history with Lucas Dean from diapers to death. Every little interaction we'd ever had was covered with a nitpicking level of detail that had me wanting to scream and crack sarcastic jokes.

But I'd promised Matt, so I was succinct and sincere and articulate and straight-forward and everything a good little witness should be.

It's fascinating really, how much of police interrogation can be driven by the perceptions of the people in the room. Did they trust me? Did I trust them? Did they really think I'd done it or were they just checking boxes? Did I have something to hide or did I feel I could be completely honest with them?

All of that goes into an interview. Into the way the questions are asked, the answers are given (or not given), and the direction the conversation takes.

Fortunately for me I trusted Matt and so did Officer Clark, so it was more formality than genuine attempt to break a suspect.

As Matt walked me towards the exit past the four desks, two facing each other on each side of the room, I saw that Jack and Trish were sitting in two of the three small plastic chairs against the front wall in the "waiting area" past the reception desk. They sat like strangers, not looking at each other, arms crossed, bodies tensed.

Matt glanced towards his brother, but turned his attention on Trish. "Come on, Trish, it's your turn."

She too glanced towards Jack as she stood and followed Matt, but Jack never once took his attention from the spot on the floor in front of his feet that he was glaring at. I waved Mason off with a quick thank-you and sprawled in the seat next to Jack.

"Well, that was fun. I'd rank it right up there next to a root canal except I've never had one." I nudged him in the ribs. "Hey, at least it's not you in there this time."

He turned towards me at last, but the usual mischievous spark that I always associated with him was missing. He was just some good-looking dark-haired guy who'd found out his wife was cheating on him. (Maybe not physically, but she certainly hadn't been honoring their relationship.)

I bit my lower lip. "Look, Jack, it's not my place, yeah? I know that. But there's this thing that happens when you're usually the person on the outside of relationships looking in like I was for most of my life. You start to see certain patterns. Certain paths relationships go down on a regular basis. And for you guys…"

He continued to stare at me, neither encouraging nor denying me.

"Well, there's this Jim Croce song. And it's not a popular one but it was on his 40th anniversary collection or whatever. And it talks about this guy who's working non-stop to build this woman he loves a castle or something. I don't know. I'm not good at describing this. But the song is about how he's off trying to give her everything in the world he thinks she deserves and all she actually wants is him to be there with her. She's lonely and feels trapped all alone at home. So I don't know. Maybe think about it. I know you want to have the money to expand the trailer so you guys can have everything you want in life, but maybe all she really wants is you."

He sat back in his chair. "Or maybe I'm just not the man who can give her everything she wants. Not without a lottery win." He scuffed his foot on the ground.

We both spared a silent moment for the story that had been on the news a couple nights before about someone in the county buying a winning lottery ticket worth over a million bucks. Whoever it was, they hadn't come forward yet. Must be nice to have that kind of windfall.

But that's not life. I long ago learned that if I was going to get anything in life it was going to be through hard work and hard choices.

So I elbowed him in the ribs. Hard.

"Ow," he grunted. "What'd you do that for?

"So you'd quit being a self-pitying idiot. You are great with Sam and a helluva lot better catch than Trish deserves. All I'm saying is maybe dial back the working all hours of the day for a bit. Don't give the Lucas Deans of the world a chance to snake their way in there."

"Do you think she did it?" he asked.

"No. Do you?"

He shook his head. "Did you ever see them together while she was living with you?"

"Not in the way you're thinking. They'd stand six feet apart at the fence edge and talk a lot, but I never saw them cross that line. I know that can still feel like a betrayal, but...People come through these things. Sometimes stronger than ever."

He leaned his head back against the wall. "I don't know who I am these days, Maggie. I used to know. I was the fast-talking con man who could get anything he wanted if you gave him enough room to operate. But now...Now I'm just some guy who works construction and comes home to sit on the couch and watch TV and drink a beer. I have a wife and kid now. I never...I don't know."

I didn't know what to tell him. The "your old life would land you in jail eventually" argument didn't seem all that convincing in the moment.

"Maybe you need to find a sales job," I suggested.

"A sales job?" He gave me a skeptical look.

"Yeah. Cars, real estate, tractors."

"Tractors?"

"I was just trying to think of big ticket items you could sell here in the valley. Once things open back up that is. I mean, you could take all that fast-talking charm that used to get you into so much trouble and apply it to making sales instead. Ethically, please. No selling lemons to some poor old lady looking for a reliable car to drive around in during the winter. But...Something that lets you shine for who you are. Construction isn't going to do that. Put those amazing people skills you have to use somehow."

"I'm an ex-con, Maggie."

"So? I've known ex-cons who were car salesmen. And brokers. You could sell investments to people. Ethically."

He grinned and I saw a little spark of the old Jack. "Ethically."

"Yes, please. I like having you around."

He leaned his head back against the wall. "I'll think about it."

"Alright. Good." I nudged him in the shoulder. "I'll see you later. Hope you're not here too long, but they're being annoyingly thorough in there."

As I made my way back home I wondered who had killed Lucas Dean. And why. I had no interest in actually investigating the murder, I was glad he was gone. But I was curious.

CHAPTER 11

After that things settled down for a few days. The cops were convinced enough that it wasn't me or Trish who'd killed Luke, but they didn't really have a good lead on who else it might've been. Turns out Luke hadn't really been seeing anyone. Or if he had there was no sign of it on his phone or email.

Basically it was all at a dead end and well on its way to being a cold case.

Until they found the second body. And then suddenly we had a real killer in our midst.

I found out about it when Matt came home that day from work. He barely gave me a kiss before walking around the house, checking all the windows to make sure they were locked.

(Of course they were. I'm a paranoid freak, so not only were they locked, they were closed with heavy curtains keeping anyone from looking inside. I'm not sure I've ever had a stalker, but if I have they didn't get to see much. My mom was always big on wide-open windows that you could see out of. Made me shudder. Because any window you can see out of, someone else can see in. If it weren't for Fancy I'd also lock the front and back door at all times.)

"What are you doing?" I asked as he finally reached the living room where I was curled up with a good book I'd been about to finish before he got home. (So close. Loved him. But. Having another person I had to give my time was seriously crimping my reading style.)

"Just making sure the house is secure," he said.

"Because the hundred-and-forty-pound black dog isn't going to deter someone?"

He glanced at Fancy who was sprawled on her back, one leg sticking up in the air, snoring. She hadn't even budged when he came home. "Not someone who's determined enough."

"Well by that standard what good is a locked window going to do? One big rock and it's all over anyway. Look, if someone wants to kill me they're going to kill me. I long ago accepted that the only reason I'm alive is because there is no one out there who really wants me dead bad enough to make it happen."

"Maggie!"

I shrugged. "What? It's true. Think about it."

"I'd rather not."

"Okay. Don't. Doesn't change the fact that it's true." I put my book aside and stood up. "Now. Why did you just go around the entire house and check that all the windows are locked?"

He crossed his arms and scanned the room one more time. "There was another murder last night."

"Same killer?" I asked.

He nodded.

"How do you know?"

"Well, same method at least. One single thrust of a knife to the right kidney."

I glanced at my bookshelf where I could see the copy of **On Killing** I'd recently finished reading. "Huh. Well, that is one of the quickest and quietest ways to kill someone. But you wouldn't expect the average person to know that."

He frowned at me. "How do **you** know that?"

I shrugged. "I read it in a book about killing people. It stuck with me."

"You read a book about killing people?" The look he gave me said he didn't believe me, but he should have known me better than that.

"Mmhm," I answered happily.

"Maggie..."

"Hey, you chose to marry me, buddy. Which means that you get the whole package, as crazy as it may be. But for what it's worth—because you are a cop after all—I'm not quite sure where the kidney is actually located, so even though I theoretically know that it can be done I wouldn't be able to actually do it, so I'm still not your killer."

"Good to know." He sank down on the couch with another sidelong look my way.

"So who was it? Who was killed?" I asked, thinking of the guy I'd seen at Luke's house before the party.

"That's the weirdest part. It was Agnes Rockmorton."

"But she's like eighty. What does an eighty-year-old woman who goes to church three times a week have in common with a philandering schmuck half her age?"

"Good question." He gave me one of his interrogator looks. "And one that the **police** will find the answer to."

I gave him back my best smile and patted him on the arm. "I'm sure you will, dear. I have every faith in you."

But my mind was already turning.

What did Agnes Rockmorton have in common with Lucas Dean other than living in Creek? And what kind of person would know how to knife someone in the kidneys? There couldn't be all that many people who fit that description could there?

Hmm. I knew Matt had said to leave it to the police, but it wouldn't hurt to poke around a little bit, would it?

CHAPTER 12

Fortunately for me, the perfect opportunity to find out more presented itself the very next day when Lesley called and asked if I'd be willing to help the Ladies' Auxiliary with the annual library fundraiser. She was hosting a lunch meeting at her house and asked if I'd like to come. Everyone was going to bring a salad and we were going to figure out what needed to happen and who would do what since it was right around the corner and not much had been done yet.

I, of course, said yes even though Fancy gave me the absolute saddest look when I blocked her inside. (If I'd been home all she would've done is sleep against the wall in the entryway, but because I was leaving, suddenly I was depriving her of the great outdoors. And I just knew when I came home she'd immediately run outside and stay there until suppertime, asserting her right to be outside no matter how miserably hot it was.)

Ah well, too bad. I didn't trust her and that picket fence. She's not much for jumping, but no point in taking any chances.

So I blocked her in and headed to Lesley's with a bowl of potato salad as an offering. I'd made it using my grandma's recipe which meant it was a full-fat version of delicious, creamy, tanginess.

By the time I pulled up outside Lesley's two-story home on the edge of town, her driveway and half the street was full of cars. As I walked up the front steps I could see why she wouldn't want to move. My grandpa's house was nice, but hers had gorgeous rose bushes that had probably taken over a decade to cultivate and a unique little rock garden off to the side with delightful gnomes tucked among the flowers.

It was clear to any observer that whoever lived there loved their home very much.

I didn't even have a chance to knock before Jolene Paige opened the door and gestured me inside. She was an incredibly slender older woman who always made me think about a passage I'd once read in a book about a woman who'd chosen, when she reached a certain age, to gain a few pounds to round out her face.

Jolene Paige had clearly never read that book. She was a bit cadaverous.

"What's that you brought? Is it potato salad? Is that **bacon** you put in there?" She looked at me wide-eyed.

"Yes."

"Oh my. Ladies," she turned to the rest of the room, "Maggie has brought the most sinful potato salad. It has bacon in it."

"Bacon?" Patrice Cole asked. She was equally slender and reminded me of some sort of little bird the way she was slightly stooped and always picked at everything she ate. "Oh dear. Well, you may have some leftovers there, Maggie."

"Because of bacon? Are you all vegetarians?"

The two women tittered at each other as I took the bowl of potato salad over to Lesley. "Did I do something wrong?" I whispered as I placed it on the table with all the other food.

"No." Lesley smiled. "Ignore them. Help yourself. We're about to get started."

There was such a wide variety of salads to choose from it was kind of amazing. Some were your standard green-lettuce salads with carrots and tomatoes, but there was also a dessert-style salad that probably had some name like pistachio ambrosia.

Not wanting to be rude—even though I'm really not a salad person and would probably have a snack when I got home—I loaded my plate up with a little bit of each one.

By the time I gingerly piled one of Lesley's chocolate brownies on top, I was wondering if the plate was going to hold up or not. Paper plates are not always the most sturdy and Lesley didn't have those plastic frames you can get to put them in that make them hold up better, but I managed by putting both hands under the plate as I wove my way to an open chair with an empty TV tray next to it.

Only when I had seated myself did I realize I was sitting next to Jolene Paige.

She leaned over and whispered to me, "You know, as you get older it gets harder to keep those pounds off, but I've managed to do so all these years with one very simple little trick."

"Really?" I took a defensive bite of brownie. "And what's that?"

"I never have a meal that's larger than the size of my fist." She proudly displayed her fist for me with a confident nod.

I tried to hide my horror. "Your fist?"

"That's right. My fist."

I looked at my own fist which was about a fifth the size of the plate I'd just sat down with. "So do you have a lot of meals throughout the day then? I've heard that's better for maintaining steady glucose levels."

"Oh no. I only have three meals. And no dessert. Ever." She glared at my brownie.

I took another bite and swallowed. "So all you eat every single day of your life is three fistfuls of food?"

"Yes. And look." She ran her hand down her side where there wasn't a sign of a curve in sight.

"Huh. How interesting. If you'll excuse me? I forgot to grab a Coke."

I left my plate and fled for the kitchen before my face could betray my absolute horror at the thought of living such a deprived life. I didn't care if that fistful of food included lobster mac 'n' cheese and tenderloin steak bites, there was no way on this earth that I would ever be happy eating just three fistfuls of food a day.

I stared at my fist again as I stepped into the kitchen.

"I see Jolene shared her diet tip with you." Lesley handed me an ice-cold can of Coke.

"She did." I shuddered. "I'm glad you don't feel that way about food. It's...disturbing. And now I have to go sit down next to her while I eat that whole plate of food. She's not going to like that very much. But good thing is, I don't care. I like food too much to listen to someone crazy like that."

Lesley patted me on the shoulder. "She means well. But I've had to sit down every one of her granddaughters over the years and explain that's not a healthy way to approach food."

"Glad someone's making the effort. Those poor kids."

I made my way back to the living room and sat down next to Jolene who stared at the Coke in my hand like it was a deadly viper.

"You don't drink diet?" she asked, scandalized.

"No. No, I do not." I took a nice, long sip and settled in for the meeting.

CHAPTER 13

One incredibly painful hour later, the business portion of the meeting was over and I'd polished off every bite on my plate even though a few of those salads had been potentially inedible. And, I am happy to report, there wasn't a drop of my potato salad left. Or any brownies, for that matter, although that could've been because I'd had three myself.

As the ladies sipped coffee and relaxed into casual gossip, I asked Jolene, "Did you know Agnes Rockmorton? Wasn't she a member of the Auxiliary before she passed?"

"Oh, I've known Agnes since we were in school together. I actually dated her late husband Theodore for two years before he went to the war. But by the time he came back I'd met my Charlie and so Theodore and Agnes fell in love. Our kids weren't quite the same age, but mine would babysit hers when they were growing up."

"I can't believe someone killed her."

Jolene gave me a look of surprise and then took a long sip of her coffee. "Oh, yes, right. Neither can I. Can you Patrice?" she asked Patrice who was seated on her other side.

Patrice leaned closer. "Mm. No. Can't imagine. She was always so nice and friendly."

I glanced back and forth between them. Something was off. "But?" I asked.

Patrice scooted her chair closer and made a point of looking around to see if anyone was listening in on us. "Well, my mom told me something very important once. She told me that there's a difference between being nice and being kind."

I let that one stew around in my brain for a minute, but didn't quite get the point. "And Agnes was…"

"She was nice. But she was not kind."

When I still looked confused, she leaned closer and continued, "For example. I never in fifty years had an unpleasant conversation with Agnes. Not once. She was always very friendly. Very cheerful. Never said a mean word about anyone. Always **nice**."

"But not kind?" I asked, still confused.

"No. Not kind. Two years ago my husband, Paul, fell and broke his hip. It made getting around very difficult. We have a side entrance to our house that doesn't have any stairs, and it was much easier for my husband to use than the front porch, which has two. But to access the side entrance required being able to drive across a portion of Agnes's driveway where she normally parked her RV. I went to her house, I explained what had happened, and I told her we'd like to be able to park Paul's van at the side of our house for a few months while he recovered. I even told her she could park her RV at the end of our property if she'd like. An RV I will add, that she had not even used since her husband died."

I nodded, still not seeing the problem.

"She informed me that she really didn't want to park her RV that far away from her house. So I asked her if she could perhaps move it farther up her driveway so that we could squeeze by. She responded that where the RV was parked was the best place for it because it was well-shaded. So I offered to buy her an RV cover. She said she'd think about it. All very nice and pleasant. Not a harsh word from her. But at the end of the day did she move that RV? No. No, she did not. See? Nice, but not kind."

I glanced at Jolene. "She was the same with you?"

"Oh yes. I still remember when we were raising money for the McKenzie's after their house burned down. She was perfectly sympathetic to Mrs. McKenzie and told her how horrible it must've been and how she hoped everything would be okay, but when I asked her to contribute a small amount to the funds we were raising to help them, she refused. Said she already had her charities she supported and couldn't possibly spare another penny."

Patrice barked a laugh. "Is that the same year she bought that absurd fur coat?"

"The exact same."

The two ladies gave each other satisfied smirks.

"Wow," I said. "So she was nice, but not kind. Friendly to someone's face, but never actually cared about anyone. That's probably the type of person who has a few enemies. But would anyone be upset enough with her to kill her?"

Jolene shrugged one shoulder and took another sip from her cup. Only then did I realize she wasn't drinking coffee, she was drinking hot water with a lemon slice in it. I wondered then if maybe she and Patrice weren't the best possible judges of, well, sanity, but hey, they were talking to me about Agnes so I was going to take what I could get.

I leaned closer and glanced around to make them think I was about to share my own big secret. "You know, my husband is working on the investigation of her murder."

"Is he?" Jolene asked as they both leaned closer.

"And he says her murder has something to do with the murder of Lucas Dean." I gave them a significant look.

"Really?" Patrice tilted her head to the side, thinking. "Well, he was doing some work for her last month."

"Was he?" I asked.

"Oh yes." She nodded. "It was quite unusual. Because he didn't have any of his normal work crew with him. It was just him. Well, him and Johnny Duffy. I saw them both there once. But Luke was there by himself every day for at least a week."

"Inside or outside?" I asked.

"Inside. But I notice things. Partially because she moved that RV for him so he could park alongside our house and not be seen from the street. So when I saw that there was a truck parked where she wouldn't let my husband park, I made a point of keeping an eye out to see who it was.

And it was Lucas Dean, but not in his normal truck."

"Huh. That's very interesting."

"Isn't it, though?" she nodded.

We all exchanged conspiratorial looks. "I'll definitely have to tell my husband about this," I said.

They both nodded in agreement and the conversation shifted towards Matt's and my wedding and married life, but the whole time I was wondering what secret project Luke could've been working on that had gotten both him and Agnes killed.

Buried treasure? Hidden body? The possibilities were endless.

CHAPTER 14

That night Matt was actually home for dinner for the first time in ages. I'd never really thought before about the challenges of being married to a cop, but it made sense that he'd be at work more during the hours when people generally get into the most trouble.

It was mid-summer and hot enough outside that I didn't want a heavy meal, but I'd had enough of salad to last a lifetime, so I made BLTs with a pesto mayo and added carrots and potato chips on the side. (I was getting fancy with that mayo, but, hey, Matt was home. And I wanted to do something nice for him.)

I tried giving Fancy one of the carrots on her sharing plate and she immediately spit it out. She'd started doing that lately. It seemed she only liked cooked carrots anymore not raw ones. But she was all about the bread and bacon and sat at my feet slowly slobbering a puddle as she waited for me to give her a bite or two.

After we'd settled into our meal and exchanged the normal "how was your day" questions, Matt cleared his throat and looked at me, his expression serious. I thought he was going to lecture me for going to the Ladies' Auxiliary meeting and asking about Agnes Rockmorton, but what he said instead took me completely by surprise.

"Maggie, I was wondering when you were going to legally change your name. We've been married a few months now and, well…It's time."

I blinked in surprise. "But I'm not going to change my name. Ever."

"We're married now."

"I understand that. But it's a new century and women don't always change their names when they get married." I tensed, realizing this might be our first fight where there was no mutually satisfying solution.

"Is it because you think we won't last?" he asked, softly.

"Oh please. I mean, if there weren't other reasons, that would be a good one. Because I have seen far too many friends think something was going to last and then find that it didn't and have to go through the rigmarole of changing things back or finding a new last name, and that is not fun. And if I were still in the working world I'd most definitely not change it professionally because no one's business what I'm doing in my personal life—especially if I were getting divorced. But that's not why."

"What is it then?"

I shook my head. "See, this is the problem with getting married before you really know someone well. Although, I guess there would be no way for you to really know this because it would've never come up."

"Maggie?" he said, his look telling me to get on with it already.

I sighed. "You know my grandpa is my step-grandpa."

"Yes. And?"

"He didn't actually marry my grandma until after my dad was grown up."

"What does that have to do with you changing your name?"

"Well...Did it never occur to you that Carver isn't the last name I was born with? Because Lou Carver wasn't my dad's real dad?"

He stared at me in complete surprise. Guess it hadn't. "So how did you end up with the last name of Carver?"

"After my parents died, the only family I had left were my grandma and my grandpa." I looked at the ceiling trying not to cry. "I missed having that family connection. I missed my parents and I wanted some clear way to show the connection I still had to my grandparents. So...I asked my grandpa if I could take on his last name."

Matt frowned at me, still confused. "But what about your original last name? Your dad's last name?"

"My dad's last name was meaningless anyway. I mean, sure,

I'd grown up with it, but he'd been adopted when he was little so it wasn't some family name that stretched back generations or anything. It was just the last name of some random dude that my grandma married for a year or so."

"Oh. I didn't know that."

"And you weren't meant to. You were just meant to think that Lou Carver is my grandpa. Because he is." I smiled, remembering. "I can't tell you how proud my grandpa was when I asked to take on his last name. He almost cried and you know Lou Carver doesn't cry much. And I know you and I are married now and that my taking your last name matters to you, but there's just no way I'm changing it. Not a chance in hell while my grandpa is still alive. And probably not after that either, to be honest."

I watched the emotions flit across Matt's face. There was disappointment at first, sure, and some sadness, but then he nodded. "I understand. And I respect that."

So many reasons I loved that man.

"You could change your last name to Carver..." I suggested. "There was a guy I knew in college whose last name was Smith who changed it to some really long, complex German name when he got married because he and his wife both shared an ancestor with that name, so it's not unheard of for a man to change his name."

He laughed. "No. I'm good with Barnes. And Barnes **is** a long-standing family name with hundreds of years of history behind it."

I clasped my hands together, pleased to have that over with. "Okay, then. Let's talk murder. Guess what I found out today?"

"Maggie..." Matt gave me that look that said he wasn't pleased, I assumed with what I wanted to talk about not my changing the subject.

"What?" I looked back at him as innocently as I could. (Which wasn't much.) "I heard some gossip that might help your investigation. Do you not want to know? Do you not want to catch the killer in our midst?"

He leaned back and took a long sip of his beer. "Go ahead. Tell me what you found."

I did. And then I asked, "Who is Johnny Duffy?"

He winced. "A low-life friend of Luke's. I don't know why he would've been at Agnes's house if Luke was doing any sort of construction work. He's not that kind of guy."

"Maybe Luke found something during his work and he called Duffy over to check it out. Like hidden gold or something."

"And then Duffy killed them both so he could have the gold himself?" Matt asked, his voice full of skepticism.

I shrugged. "It's possible. There was gold mining in Colorado at one point."

"I'm pretty sure people didn't go around hiding gold in their walls, even back then."

"Hey. Don't mock a viable theory. Maybe it wasn't gold. Maybe it was bearer bonds. Or cash. Or a dead body. I don't know. But you have to admit, knowing that Luke was doing work at Agnes's house before they were both killed helps."

He took another swig of his beer. "It does. I won't deny it. But..."

"Stay out of it." I rolled my eyes.

He nodded. "Exactly.

I changed the subject, but that didn't mean my mind stopped working through the possibilities. You can't set me a puzzle and then expect that I won't try to solve it. That's not how my mind works. I'll keep worrying at it like a dog with a bone until I figure it out. Or until someone gives me the answer.

So all Matt had to do was find the killer first and I'd stop trying to solve the murder. But until then...I was going to keep thinking about who the murderer could be and why they'd killed two very different people.

I decided, though, that for the sake of marital harmony Matt didn't need to know I was still **thinking** about it. As long as I didn't **do** anything, that should be acceptable. Right? Right.

CHAPTER 15

Of course, life likes to mock my decisions, so the very next day when I went to the grocery store I saw that jerk who'd been setting off fireworks at Luke's house the week he was killed.

"Whatchoo looking at?" he grunted at me as I studied him from the checkout line.

I pointed at him. "You were at Lucas Dean's house, helping him set up for his party on the third."

"I was. And?"

"We were never properly introduced." I held out my hand. "Maggie May Carver."

He looked at it like I was holding out a deadly snake. "People aren't supposed to be shaking hands anymore. It's not safe."

I raised an eyebrow, surprised to have this Neanderthal of a man telling me about public health and safety. "Fair enough. But you are?"

"Johnny."

"Johnny Duffy?" I asked, suddenly excited.

"Yeah." He narrowed his eyes at me. "What's it to you?"

I pulled my cart out of line and stepped closer to him, but not too close. (Public safety and all.)

"Is it true you were helping Luke out with whatever he was working on over at Agnes Rockmorton's house?" I asked, studying him carefully.

He stepped back as if I'd shot him and glanced around. "I had nothing to do with that."

"With what?" I asked.

"You know."

"No. I'm afraid I don't. I just heard that Luke was doing some work over there and that you were with him one day. What was he working on?" I tilted my head to the side, waiting eagerly for his reply.

Johnny licked his lips nervously and looked around. "Nothing."

"Nothing? He was there every day for an entire week. And you say it's nothing. What did you do over there?" I stepped closer.

He stepped back. "I just helped him move a few things he couldn't move on his own."

"But I heard you weren't the construction type. And, pardon my saying it, it seems to me Luke had a bunch of guys working for him more capable of moving something heavy around than you."

He glared at me, but didn't deny the fact. "Luke and I go way back. He trusted me."

I smiled, triumphant. "So he was moving things around he didn't want people to know about?"

Johnny shook his head slightly and stepped away from me. "I gotta go. I'm gonna be late."

He turned and walked right for the exit, leaving his grocery cart behind, Hungry Man frozen dinners and all. I was tempted to run after him, but instead I got back in line and checked out. But the whole time I was wondering what Luke and Agnes had been up to that had spooked Johnny Duffy so bad he couldn't even talk to me about it.

CHAPTER 16

When I returned home I tried to forget about Johnny Duffy and the murders. I had faith in Matt and his team. They'd figure out what was going on eventually. But, well, you know me. I was home and bored and there was a murderer on the loose. If they'd kill an old lady, who knows who else they'd kill. And I had people I cared about.

(I know. Most murderers don't just run around killing people willy-nilly, so the odds that someone I loved was actually in danger were pretty slim. But they weren't zero. Which gave me enough of an excuse to justify poking around a bit more.)

I figured there was no harm in taking Fancy for her walk the next morning in the direction of Agnes

Rockmorton's house instead of towards the ballpark. Variety is good, right? Give her something new to look at. Some new scents to explore.

And give me a good excuse to maybe poke around a bit. That early I didn't expect anyone else to be up and about.

But I'd underestimated the early-bird nature of Patrice Cole, her next door neighbor. Patrice was out in her garden pulling weeds as Fancy and I walked up. The two houses sat side-by-side on twin lots backed up against the side of the mountain, a dirt alleyway running between them and no fences in sight. Agnes's house was painted a brick red, Patrice's a disturbing shade of light green, but otherwise they looked identical—smaller homes on medium-sized plots of land with green lawns and a border of flowers that ran along the street side.

"Morning, Patrice," I called, stopping far enough away Fancy couldn't step on her begonias. (Or whatever they were. I'm not a flower expert. I know a rose and a tulip and a daisy and then after that it's all just one giant blur of "that red flower" or "that purple flower.")

"Morning, Maggie. How are you today?" She was positively radiant, grinning from ear to ear.

"Good." I glanced towards Agnes's house. "I see the RV is gone."

"Well..." She nodded towards the far end of the street where I could see an RV parked. "Paul and I figured Agnes wasn't going to mind if we repositioned it a bit. He can manage the front steps fine these days but that hip still gives him a bit of trouble now and then so it's best to be able to come in through the back."

"You towed it?" I tried to keep the surprised judgement out of my voice, but probably failed.

"Hardly. I knew where she kept the keys, so Paul just borrowed them for a moment." She pulled out another weed with a vindictive little smile on her face and more force than was necessary.

I tilted my head to the side, trying to make sure I was understanding her. "So to be clear. Your husband walked into your dead neighbor's house and borrowed her keys so he could move her RV to a more suitable location?"

"Yes." She nodded sharply, smiling.

"Wasn't the house locked?"

She waved that question away. "Oh, we've had a spare key for a number of years now. Just in case, you know. We were all very close. We'd water their plants when Ted and Agnes traveled. And they'd water ours. Better than relying on our unreliable offspring."

I've always found it mildly disturbing the thought of having someone else in my home when I'm not there. It's why I'd never pay for a house cleaner because the thought of someone else touching my things when I'm not around is more upsetting to me than having a quarter-inch of dust on everything.

(Not that it ever gets **that** bad. But visible dust is not unknown.)

I shook off thoughts of privacy and dusting and focused in on what really mattered. "Patrice, do you think you might be willing to let me use that key to maybe poke around a bit inside? I'm still trying to figure out what kind of work Lucas Dean was doing in her home. I ran into Johnny Duffy the other day and he ran out of the store when I tried to talk to him about it."

She pressed her lips together and studied me while I held my breath and silently prayed she'd agree.

She looked at Fancy with a frown. "We can't take the dog inside. I don't really want to explain to the cops about having that key. They might reach the wrong conclusions."

"Right..."

"But you can leave it with Paul and I'll go over there with you."

"Okay."

I wanted to tell her not to refer to my dog as an "it" but I didn't want her to change her mind, so I just led Fancy after her as she took us in through the back door. Paul Cole was sitting at the kitchen table with a cup of coffee and a copy of the local newspaper. He was a robust man and reminded me of a grandpa-type from a late 80's sitcom, weird mustache and all. Someone with a name like Willard.

Their kitchen was nice enough. Nothing special. Linoleum and wood cabinets, but well-kept, bright, and homey.

"Paul, I'm going to take Maggie next door to Agnes's house. Keep an eye on the dog."

I added, "She might bark a little when I leave, but she's a big fan of bacon and cheese and eggs and bread." I nodded towards his plate. "Hold up a piece of any of that and she'll come right to attention. Just don't do it too long unless you want a giant puddle of drool on the floor."

He eyed Fancy who was standing next to me because I still had her on leash. "Never much liked dogs."

"Well, this one's an exception. And we won't be gone long." I let her off the leash and she made a beeline for the table and started sniffing around. "Fancy, be good."

She glanced at me and then sat down, expectantly waiting, her attention focused on Paul Cole and his plate of deliciousness.

"Be back soon, Fancy" I said as I stepped back outside, following after Agnes.

Fancy whirled around, looking like I'd just told her I was leaving forever and would never ever come back, ever.

"Fifteen minutes, Fancy. Fifteen minutes, that's all." I closed the door and walked quickly away before I could let her heartbroken cries get to me. I couldn't pass up this opportunity. I had to see what Lucas Dean had been working on in Agnes Rockmorton's house and this might be my one and only chance to get inside.

CHAPTER 17

Patrice glanced both ways before quickly opening the front door and letting me in. "Hurry up now," she said, hustling me along so she could shut the door immediately behind us.

"We're not doing anything wrong. You have a key," I said.

"Yes, but I'd rather no one knew that."

I was tempted to ask why, but then I might not get a chance to look around, so I let it slide. Better that than remind her that I was in fact married to a cop.

"So," I said. "You've been here many times before, what looks different? What could Lucas Dean have been working on here for a week?"

Patrice led me through a living room decorated with one too many crocheted doilies. Don't get me wrong, I like a good crocheted doily myself, but when there's one under every single bowl and vase and figurine, it gets to be a bit much. That's why I don't crochet all that much anymore, those things multiply faster than rabbits given the chance.

"She was quite the crafter," I said to have something to say.

Patrice glared at a little table full of crystal figurines and beige doilies edged in forest green. "Mm. She was."

"You didn't like her work?" I asked.

She pursed her lips. "I liked it fine. But every single Christmas the woman gave me something else. And I've known her since the 70's. Fifty years of **this**." She hissed the last word as she gestured around the room. "And if I didn't put them all out, she noticed. **Where's that tablecloth I made you, Patrice? Where's that afghan I made you, Patrice?** Sometimes a woman just wants to use a nice store-bought blanket."

I raised my eyebrows at her vehemence. "It sounds like you guys had an interesting friendship."

She grunted but changed the subject. "Living room looks the same as always."

As we walked through the rest of the main level she confirmed that all of the rooms looked unchanged as far as she could tell. The whole house was decorated in beige, peach, and green; Patrice confirmed that's how it had always been.

"Fifty years and the woman never changed things up."

I bit my lip to keep from commenting again. "If nothing's changed then what was Lucas Dean working on?"

Patrice exhaled loudly through her nose as she stared at a door tucked away at the end of the kitchen, her lips pressed tight together. "Maybe she finally got rid of the fun room." She pronounced the fun in fun room like it was anything but.

"The fun room?" I asked, feeling a little scared about what I might learn.

"Come along. Either you'll see or you won't."

She jerked open the door and led me down a narrow set of stairs into what looked to me to be a very normal and boring basement other than the fact that it was completely empty. There was a long bar at one end of the room with beer steins lined up along glass shelves and stools set up in front of it. But nothing else. No couches, no television. Just bare concrete floor.

It certainly didn't meet my definition of fun.

Patrice looked around and nodded. "Well, that explains it."

"What?"

"She must've had him remove the fun room. She'd want some discretion for that. Probably why he had Johnny Duffy help with the heavy lifting rather than his usual crew. Johnny Duffy is a lot of things, but he's most definitely not one to talk out of turn."

"Patrice, you keep referring to it as the fun room. Dare I ask what that means?"

She crossed her arms and glared at me. "What do you think it means?"

"I don't know. That's why I'm asking."

(I actually had my suspicions, but I wasn't just going to blurt them out. What if I was wrong? This was an eighty-year-old woman we were talking about.)

"Well, do you think we played **Bingo** down here? Because we didn't."

"Okay. What..." I really didn't want to finish that sentence. I really didn't want to know. I understand that everyone has a history and that sometimes that history is quite...interesting. But I prefer to think of my little old ladies as always having been little old ladies and not swinging singles from the 70's, you know?

Patrice stood her ground, hands on hips, daring me to ask. I changed my tactics.

"Um, whatever was down here, would there be anything about it that would make someone kill two people over it?" I asked instead.

"No. Only thing about down here that might make someone kill someone is the memories."

"Uh...what memories?" I kinda winced as I asked the question.

"Where do you think we got her house key from?" Patrice huffed at me before turning and making her way back up to the kitchen.

I did not need that visual in my mind. No, no, I did not.

(Which is not to say that I am judging anyone who has ever participated in one of those key parties. You do you. But it's just so contrary to my possessive nature that I can't go there easily. To think about going to a party with Matt and then...NO. MINE. HANDS OFF. And I'd like to think he'd feel the same way.)

As I followed Patrice back up the stairs I wondered if she was the type of person to hold a grudge over something like that. I knew I was, but was she? Could that initial encounter have led to years of resentment and increasing hostility until she'd finally decided to knife Agnes Rockmorton in the back?

Maybe. But then why kill Luke first? Had he found out about who participated in the fun room? Maybe he'd tried to blackmail Patrice and it failed and then Patrice was so mad at Agnes for giving away her secret that she killed her, too?

Eh. I couldn't exactly picture the bird-like little woman in front of me knifing someone in the kidneys. Saying something nasty behind their back, absolutely. But killing them? No. That would have to be Paul Cole. And why would he do it? To protect his reputation? Or because his wife told him to?

No. Plus, killing someone to keep a secret has never made much sense to me. What better way for something like that to become public knowledge than to kill two people over it and have it revealed to the world as the motive at your trial?

Then again, not many people think of that sort of thing when it comes to murder. They kill to protect the secret first and only later realize that the murder itself is much more likely to reveal the secret than the person they killed ever was.

Hm.

I wasn't sure it made sense. But I wasn't ready to rule it out yet either.

So good news was I had at least one suspect. Bad news was I was never going to get the idea of Agnes Rockmorton who crocheted beige and maroon dollies but also had a fun room in her basement out of my head.

Or the idea of Patrice or Paul Cole reaching into a paper bag to retrieve a random person's keys and take them home.

Worse yet—because there was nothing left in the fun room anymore—I was left to imagine what had been there before. And I have an unfortunately good imagination...

Yikes.

CHAPTER 18

I thanked Patrice profusely for her help and went back with her to retrieve Fancy who was curled up at Paul Cole's feet, her gaze fixed on the kitchen door just waiting for me to return. Not that she made a mad scramble to reach my side once we walked in the door, she was too annoyed at me for that.

Instead she lay by his side and glared at me until I reached into my bag and pulled out a nice little bribe. I never leave home without copious amounts of treats for Fancy. It's easier to lure her with a tasty salmon snap than rely on her actually obeying me voluntarily.

"Nice dog," Paul Cole grunted as Fancy scrambled to her feet.

"Told you she was special." I nodded at his arm. "Nice tattoo you have there. What is it?"

He glanced at his arm. "From my Army days. Long time ago now. We all got drunk one night and got matching tattoos."

"It's important to commemorate something like that."

He snorted. "Not sure it was worth the lecture we got the next morning. Or how they ran us until we puked our guts out the next three days in a row."

I frowned at his reaction, but didn't say anything else about it, just gathered up Fancy and headed home. It's easy to think that all members of a military service are the same. That every Ranger or Marine or SEAL has the same core beliefs and values. That same dedication to mission and doing what's right. But that's not reality. Different people go into the military for different reasons. And not all of them are because they're good, decent human beings looking to make the world a better place.

And sometimes even the ones that go in good come out the other side broken. Which meant that Paul Cole's military background made him a more likely suspect. Far more likely than someone like Johnny Duffy who could probably fire one of those guns that blow up groundhogs with the best of them but was far less likely to know his way around lethal knife techniques.

I got home and put down Fancy's food for her before picking up my phone to follow-up on the notion that Lucas Dean was trying to blackmail Patrice Cole.

Trish answered on the third ring.

"Hey Trish, how's it going?" I asked.

"Maggie? Why are you calling me?"

It was a fair question. We hadn't exactly bonded when she and Sam were my houseguests. As a matter of fact I might have contemplated certain rash and illegal actions at more than one point while she was staying with me. How can one person watch that much reality television? How can there be that many crazy, trashy shows about people hooking up or trying to hook up? She even watched the UK ones for crying out loud.

"I had a question or two about Luke," I said.

"Ugh. I'd rather not talk about that man ever again. I spent three hours with the cops having my life picked apart. And then I got to go home and spend three more hours talking to Jack about it."

"How are you guys doing with all that, by the way?"

She sighed loudly. "Good actually. We'd never had a talk like that before. Not when we were dating the first time and not this time either. I don't know, we just assumed what the other wanted and turns out we were both wrong. Jack was working second jobs because he thought I wanted another kid, but I don't. Sam is great and I love him, but I'd like to go back to school not get pregnant again. But I thought he wanted another kid so I was gonna go along with it. But he doesn't either. He said you suggested he get a sales job, which I think would be great. So we're going to use our savings to help him start up a sales career. It's not easy those first six months. But if we don't add onto the trailer, we'll have enough to get by even if he doesn't sell anything. Worst case scenario, we can apply for help to the Valley Fund."

(The Valley Fund was the result of Greta and Mason putting their substantial financial resources towards keeping the valley safe and isolated until the current worldwide craziness was over. They were the main backers but we'd all committed to not letting anyone fall through the cracks while the valley was sealed off from the rest of the world.)

I nodded my head even though she couldn't see it. "Glad to hear it. And if I know Jack, he'll definitely make a sale in those first few months."

"I hope so."

She sounded happy about all of it and I was happy for them. Glad they'd worked through their issues and were trying to make it work. Especially for Sam's sake. Jack adored that boy and I think Sam felt the same for Jack.

"You had questions?" Trish prompted.

"Yeah. You were talking to Luke a lot right before everything happened. Did he ever mention to you what he was working on at Agnes Rockmorton's?"

(Yes, I realize I could've avoided an uncomfortable walk through her house if I'd just asked Trish, but, well, my mind doesn't always turn to the easiest solution first.)

"No. I knew he was doing work there, but not what he was doing specifically. Just that it paid well and that he used Johnny Duffy instead of his normal guys to help him move the biggest pieces out. He wasn't exactly thrilled to use Johnny. Guy's a good drinking buddy but not a hard worker."

"Did Jack seem excited to you? Like he thought he was going to come into a lot of money or anything?"

"Come to think of it...He was happy that last night at the party. That's part of why I was surprised when he didn't answer the phone when I called later. Because he told me he had big news he didn't want to share at the party. He said it was huge. Life-changing. But that he'd tell me later."

"Did you tell the cops that?"

"Yeah. But I didn't know what the news was, so I had nothing more to share. Can't really do much with someone was happy they had big life-changing news."

"Fair enough." I thought about it for a moment. "But he wasn't working at Agnes's house that week was he?"

"Oh no. He'd wrapped that up the week before, I think."

"Huh. Alright, thanks. Tell Jack hi for me."

"Will do."

I hung up the phone and stared at the wall.

I shuddered as I forced myself to think about each and every person I knew in Creek who was over the age of sixty who might've attended those parties at Agnes's house. Lesley? My grandpa? The preacher and his wife?

Ugh.

"Don't judge, Maggie," I muttered to myself. "You know darned well when you're sixty you're going to hope you and Matt are still going that strong. Or that you at least have some fun memories to look back on if you aren't."

Still. I didn't like to think about it. I preferred to imagine that all babies were delivered by storks and all marriages consisted of prim little couples sleeping in separate single beds that were made-up each morning with hospital corners.

I know. I'm weird.

The more I thought about it, though, the more the blackmail angle just didn't fit. Because even if Luke had been going to blackmail not only Patrice Cole but every other individual who'd ever used the fun room, I couldn't imagine the amount of money involved would've been enough to change his life. Maybe buy a few kegs of beer...But change a life? Mm. I didn't think so.

Still. Better to be thorough.

Wincing at what I had to do next, I leashed Fancy back up. "Come on, girl. Time to go have the most awkward conversation I have ever had in my entire life."

CHAPTER 19

As I waited at my grandpa's front door I silently prayed that he wouldn't be home. Ever again. Or at least not until after they found the murderer. But he answered almost immediately.

Great.

"Maggie May. To what do I owe the pleasure this early in the morning?" He had his glasses on so I'd probably interrupted him in the midst of doing his morning crossword puzzle.

"Can't a girl just drop in on her grandpa?" I asked, disingenuously, as I let Fancy off her leash and she ran away towards the backyard.

"She could, but she rarely does. Especially at seven in the morning. Are you out of Coke? I should still have one in the fridge." He glanced at his watch. "Is this important? Lesley will be by in a few minutes. We're going out to breakfast in Bakerstown."

Lesley. Just when I thought this couldn't get worse.

It was good for the investigation that she was coming over. But I did not want to be asking my new step-grandmother about her participation in fun room parties at Agnes Rockmorton's house.

"Well?" my grandpa asked.

I nudge my way inside. "Let's wait until Lesley gets here and then I'll explain."

He narrowed his eyes. "Are you investigating those murders? Because you don't need to. That's what the cops do."

"Grandpa."

"Don't roll your eyes at me. You know I'm right. If you are investigating those murders, stop."

I walked into the kitchen and grabbed the Coke he'd mentioned out of the fridge. "I can't just stop."

"Why not?"

I didn't answer until I'd taken a big swig of soda, letting it bite at the back of my throat in that perfect way I love so much. "I can't just turn it off, Grandpa."

"Turn what off?"

"My mind. I can't just start thinking about something like that and then stop. Haven't you ever...?" I glanced around for a good way to explain it to him. "There. Your crossword puzzle. Do you ever have a day when you don't finish? When you just set it aside undone? Like, **'Oh well, I gave it an hour and couldn't finish it, better things to do today'** and then never go back to it and never think of it again? Or do you sit with it until it's done or even come back to it the next day if you don't get a chance to finish?"

He shrugged. "If I can't solve it, I can't solve it. It goes in the trash. Life is too short to keep banging on at something forever. I work the crossword during breakfast and if I'm not done by the time breakfast is over, oh well."

I physically recoiled at that thought. "Really? You can just take a half-finished crossword and throw it in the trash?"

"Yes."

I shuddered. "See, I can't. Once I started that crossword I would have to finish it. Even if it took me four hours. Even if it took me more than a day. And if for some reason I didn't finish it, it would stick with me. My mind would keep thinking about that puzzle until I solved it. And if I never solved it, it would always be on my mind to some little degree. Seriously. Five years later, I'd be reading some book and suddenly think, **'Aha! That was the answer to 42 Down.'**"

He didn't say it, but I knew what he was thinking. That I was crazy. And maybe I was, but that was me. I can't stop trying to solve a puzzle or a problem once I start. Either I have to solve it or someone else does.

"So you're telling me that these murders are a puzzle for you? And that now that you've started thinking about them you will keep thinking about them until they're solved?"

I nodded. "Exactly. Which means the best thing to do is help me solve them so I can clear my mind and move on."

"It's your husband's job to solve the murders, not yours." He gave me his best grandpa glare.

"I know that. But..."

"Maggie May."

I pressed my lips together and stared at him, pleading. I couldn't let it go. "Please, Grandpa. Help me."

He huffed. "Fine. But this is the last one you get involved in."

I didn't answer because we both knew the only way I wasn't going to get involved in the next murder was if I didn't know about it.

Fortunately for both of us, Lesley pulled up just then.

CHAPTER 20

We settled around the kitchen table, each of them with a cup of coffee in hand and me with my Coke.

"Well, out with it," my grandpa said. "How can we help you find the murderer?"

"Did you guys know that Agnes Rockmorton had a fun room in her house?" I asked, not really wanting to.

My grandpa snorted in amusement. "Ah, Agnes and her fun room. Were you there, Lesley? At her sixtieth? When she wanted everyone to line up and..."

"Please, Grandpa. No details. Please."

He smirked at me before taking a sip of his coffee. "What do you want to know then?"

"Did anything ever happen there that was big enough it would be worth blackmailing someone for life-changing money?"

He sat back and thought about it. "There was that one time...But you don't want details."

"Oh, honestly, Lou." Lesley smacked him on the arm before turning her attention to me. "Agnes's parties weren't actually much of anything. Agnes thought she was being very wild with that fun room of hers. And, yes, I was at her sixtieth. It was nothing more than a bunch of sixty-somethings drinking too much and reminiscing about their wilder days, honestly."

"But I heard something about...keys." I winced.

My grandpa chuckled. "Oh, Agnes's key party...I'd forgotten about that one. It was about ten years ago?" He set his coffee down. "Pretty sure there were only two sets of keys in that bag that night. When Marie and I heard what she had planned we ducked out the back. And we weren't the only ones."

"So did Bill and I." Lesley shook her head. "That was the most transparent attempt I've ever seen by a woman to sleep with another woman's husband."

"Who wanted who?" I asked her.

"Agnes wanted Paul. Had for years."

"And Patrice and Theodore?"

"Went along with it. It was going to happen one way or another. Might as well know when."

I bit my lip. "Do you think they were still…?"

"What, now? No. I always had the impression it didn't go very well. That's why Agnes wouldn't move that RV when Paul was injured. A little bit of payback for leading her on for so long and then not rising to the occasion."

"Do you think Patrice or Paul could've held a grudge this long and finally killed Agnes over it?"

My grandpa answered. "No. No chance."

I finished my Coke and sat back with a frustrated sigh. "Great. I'm back at square one. All I know is that

Lucas Dean was excited about some life-changing event but from what you're telling me it had nothing to do with Agnes Rockmorton and her fun room."

"Since you're back at square one, you should let Matt handle it."

"Grandpa. I told you I can't let it go once I get started. But what I can do is tell Matt everything I've learned. Maybe he'll see something I haven't." I stood up. "Thank you guys. Enjoy your breakfast."

Even though it wasn't a part of the investigation anymore, as I left the house I couldn't help but think about what Agnes Rockmorton had asked for at her sixtieth birthday.

My mind, I swear, I'd love to be able to just turn it off some days.

CHAPTER 21

Matt was still sleeping when I returned home so I decided to clean a bit. I know, me choosing to clean voluntarily, something had to be wrong. But see, here's the weird thing. When I was on my own I really didn't care about any mess I made because I knew it was my mess and somehow that made it less of something to worry about.

But now that Matt and I were married and sharing a space, every stain I saw was potentially not my stain but his. And for some reason other people's dirt squicks me out in a way that my own doesn't. It's not rational, but it is what it is.

So I cleaned. Plus, I figured if I felt that way about things then maybe Matt did, too, and I didn't want my "ex-military, lined his shoes up parallel by the front door when he got home each night" husband, to think I was a slob.

Not for the first six months at least. I wouldn't be able to hide it forever, but I figured I could do so for at least the honeymoon period. Let him think he'd gotten a good deal for a few months at least.

When I heard the shower turn on in the master bedroom I set to making him breakfast. Nothing fancy. Just a heated up can of black beans with cumin added in, a couple fried eggs, bacon, some Greek yogurt, and salsa. It was one of my go-to breakfast choices and much more exciting than toast with peanut butter and an apple, which was my other go-to.

By the time he came into the kitchen toweling his hair dry, everything was done and on the table. I'd even put down a napkin for him.

He eyed the table suspiciously. "What have you done?"

"I made you breakfast. Can't a wife make her husband breakfast?"

He stayed where he was, narrowing his eyes at me. "**A** wife can make her husband breakfast, I'm just not sure you're that wife."

"Hey now. All you have to do is ask and I'll have a hi-ball or whatever it is ready and waiting as soon as you walk through that door each night."

He laughed and sat down. "Thank you."

"You're welcome." I sat down across from him and dropped a bit of yogurt and bacon onto Fancy's sharing plate. "So...How's work going?"

He smiled at me, like **Gotcha, I knew there was an ulterior motive**, but all he said was, "Work's good. You know I thought with the valley closed off we'd have less speeders, but the locals are making up for it."

He then launched into a five-minute-long series of stories about all the various speeders he'd had to pull over in the last few days. The stories were entertaining—I even laughed at a few—but by the end of the five minutes I was glaring at him more than laughing.

"What's wrong?" he asked, guilelessly. "I thought you wanted to hear about how work was going."

"Matt."

"Yes?"

"You know me."

He smiled. "I do."

"So...How is work going?" I stabbed my fork at a couple of black beans on the bottom of the bowl that didn't want to let me catch them.

"Oh, you mean how is the investigation into Lucas Dean's murder going?"

If looks could kill, I would've been a widow in that moment.

He laughed as he set his bowl on the floor next to Fancy for her to polish off the last little bit. When he sat back he was serious and unhappy. "Not well. We know Luke did work at Agnes's house shortly before the murders, but no one seems to know what kind of work he did for her."

"Oh, I know that."

He tilted his head to the side. "Do you now?"

"I just found out this morning, I swear." I proceeded to fill him in on my house tour and embarrassing visit with my grandpa and Lesley.

"Well, at least you got to be the one to talk to your grandpa about that. I'm afraid I'd never be able to look the man in the eye again if I had to talk to him about sex. That's a little too close to reminding him that his granddaughter and I..."

"Whoa, there. No changing the subject."

He winked at me. "Why not? I have a few hours before I have to be back on shift and we are newlyweds..."

"Matthew Allen Barnes. I am trying to catch a murderer here. Stick to the subject. You didn't know what Luke was doing at Agnes Rockmorton's house and I've now told you. Do you have any idea what life-changing news he had?"

"No. A few people commented about how excited Luke seemed that last night. Said he was talking about getting a boat he'd been wanting for ages. Someone said he mentioned sailing around the Caribbean this winter. But no one knew why he could suddenly afford it."

I stared at the ceiling, trying to think what it could be. "Drugs? Smuggling? Did you check that he hadn't established some back way into the valley because that is totally something Luke would do?"

"We're all over that, don't worry. I have no desire to face you if your grandpa gets sick because I failed to catch someone sneaking in here and bringing that illness with them."

"Okay, then. But the life-changing news definitely involved coming into some money?"

He nodded. "Seems so. He didn't tell anyone where the money was coming from or what he was going to do for it. But whatever it was, it didn't sound like a job of any sort. Because all the stories I heard from the few days before he died were that he was talking about taking vacations or buying big toys. If he was going to earn the money through work I'd assume he'd be more focused on the job than the perks."

I put my bowl on the floor for Fancy and took the one Matt had given her to the sink. "Did he have any relatives that died lately? Maybe he was due to inherit and someone killed him to get access to the money themselves. Who gets his house?"

"If someone killed him for his money, that backfired."

"Why?"

He grinned at me.

"What?"

"Luke had a will."

"And? So?"

He crossed his arms and leaned back in his chair looking far too smug. "He left every single penny he had to charity."

I snorted. "No he didn't."

"He did. Split equally between the local humane society, the Red Cross, and some group dedicated to the preservation of the rain forest."

"No. That has to be a joke. Lucas Dean and the rain forest?"

Matt shrugged one shoulder. "He'd also been supporting some charity in Africa every month. Even had a picture of the kid he'd 'adopted' on the wall in his office."

"No." I did not need to hear that at some deep level Lucas Dean was a decent human being. No. No, no, no.

Matt grinned. "Seems you misjudged him."

"I did not. No matter how many kids he saved from starvation in Africa he was still the man who set off fireworks when Fancy was right there and who broke my best friend's heart more than once."

"What can I say? Some people are complex."

I stared Matt down, waiting for him to crack and tell me it was a joke, but he didn't. I shook my head. Who knew that Lucas Dean had a heart hidden somewhere under all those layers of trouble-making jerk?

Still. Didn't make me wish he was alive. It had been far too peaceful without him living next door for that.

I glanced at the clock and then back at Matt. "Well...If there's nothing else to discuss about the case, we do have a few hours until you're due into work, and we are newlyweds after all...Perhaps..."

Matt flashed me his best grin. "Now we're talking."

CHAPTER 22

That night I went over to my grandpa's for dinner and some Scrabble. Lesley was at some sort of event for the library that he hadn't wanted to attend, so he invited me over for his famous stuffed cheeseburgers. Instead of melting the cheese on top of the meat he stuffed it into the center of the patty so that it was all yummy, gooey when I bit into it.

There is no better way to make a cheeseburger in my humble opinion.

When my grandpa played "zebra" to start the game of Scrabble off, I knew I was in trouble. It only got worse from there. By the time I pulled the last tile out of the bag I was down by fifty points and staring at a tray full of consonants without a friendly vowel in sight. About all I could find to play was "by".

But I toughed it out and went down swinging, because even when all the odds are against me I don't know how to quit. I lost by sixty-points. It was a thorough trouncing.

"Rematch?" my grandpa asked as I took a swig of my beer.

"No."

"You okay?"

"I guess. Just wondering what I'm doing with my life, that's all."

He snorted. "You kids these days. I never once stopped to think about what I was doing with my life. I just lived it. There were no plans or second-guessing, it was just life."

"Well, if you hadn't figured this out about me by now I think about everything all the time. If I'm not completely overwhelmed by what's happening, I think. And right now with the barkery shut down and the resort opening maybe never I have lots and lots and lots of time on my hands to think."

"What are you thinking about?" he asked.

"My best friend is having a kid. And...I don't know. I'm happy for her, but I don't want to be fifty-five at my kid's high school graduation, so I'm not really sure I want to follow her down that road. And I don't know how Matt will feel about that. I wish I could go back a decade in time, meet Matt then, and have a kid with him then. But to do so now?" I winced.

"I never had kids," he said with a shrug.

"And? Was that a good thing or a bad thing?"

He shook his head. "It was just life. I told you, I never planned what would happen. I just took life as it came at me and for me that meant not having kids. But I did love being around when you were little. Kids are amazing. They show you the world in a way you'll never see it on your own."

"But they're tiring. It's like Fancy on steroids. I can leave her at home for a few hours and go to the store or whatever, but do that with a toddler they'll throw you in jail. Plus, you put in all that effort and maybe they don't like you at the end of it. Or maybe they never leave. Some kids stay at home until they're like ninety these days. I can't have that."

He chuckled. "Stop worrying about things you can't control and just let it happen."

"No. I have to be in control."

"Maggie May, what makes you think you're in control of anything right now?"

I opened my mouth and then closed it. He was right. Between Fancy, Matt, and random murders my life already wasn't my own. "You are not helping, Grandpa."

"Just calling it how I see it. What else have you learned about the murders?"

"Not much. Seems Luke was talking like he was coming into money. Said he was going to buy a boat and sail around the Caribbean in it. But no one knows how he was coming into that money. Matt said it wasn't drugs or smuggling, but what else could it be? He said the way Luke was talking it wasn't an ongoing job of any sort. Sounded more like found money, like an inheritance or something. Which brings me back to Agnes Rockmorton. Maybe he found something in that basement when he dismantled it. More than just a fun room."

"Maybe. I never heard any rumors about money when it came to Agnes and Theodore. He worked in the forest service most of his life. Wasn't a gambler. Wasn't one to bend the rules in any way. And if Luke did find something there then why was **he** killed first? And why then kill Agnes?"

"To get it back? And then she was killed so she wouldn't tell anyone and whoever killed both of them could have the money free and clear?"

"Hm." He took a swig of his beer. "Not lining up for me."

"I know. Me neither."

"You sure you don't want a rematch?"

I glanced at the board. Scrabble is definitely a game of skill and my grandpa was a master, but there is that luck angle to it in terms of which tiles you draw and when, and maybe if I tried again my luck would shine through. One thing was certain, if I didn't play him again I'd never have a chance to beat him.

"Alright. One more. But I'm going to grab us both some of that key lime pie Lesley made first."

CHAPTER 23

It was almost nine when I walked Fancy and myself back home. It was a gorgeous night, absolutely still except for the sounds of crickets or whatever they were chirping in the distance. The sky was dark and clear and full of stars. It was that perfect summer mountain cool temperature that I loved. Almost needing a jacket, but not quite.

I tell ya, I'd be happy if it was sixty-five to eighty-five degrees year-round even if I did have to sacrifice the seasons to get it.

Alas. Might take a few months but winter was definitely going to come back, snow and all.

As I opened the gate and walked Fancy towards the front door, I glanced in the direction of Luke's house. Why had he been killed? What did it have to do with Agnes Rockmorton? There had to be something I was missing. What was it?

Fancy tugged on her leash and I let her go to run off behind the house. Matt wasn't due home for a few more hours. Even though we'd walled off the valley from the rest of the world, people hadn't stopped drunk driving and getting into domestic disputes.

At my wit's end, I called Greta.

"Maggie. This is a pleasant surprise. How are you?" she answered, the clipped sound of her German accent more soothing than you'd expect.

"Good."

"You do not sound good."

I plopped onto the couch with a big sigh. "You heard that Lucas Dean was killed?"

"I did. This is very sad. He was not the kind of man you marry, but he was very fun. And he did good work on my house."

"Did you keep in touch with him? After?"

She laughed once. "No."

Her answer made it clear that he'd been hired help and not the type of person she'd choose to associate with socially. I'd been fortunate that not only had she been my best customer when the barkery was open but we'd also become friends at some point along the way.

"So you wouldn't have any idea how he was going to come into a bunch of money? I was thinking maybe drugs or smuggling or something."

"No. It was not that."

"You seem very sure."

"I am. When I agreed to help seal off the valley, I also made certain arrangements to ensure that the valley remained sealed. It has. There is no smuggling. At least not now."

"Was there?"

"Eh. One or two people may have tried. They did not succeed. They are no longer trying."

The way she said that gave me pause. "Are they still alive, Greta?"

"Of course. What do you think of me, Maggie? I was a jewel thief, but never a murderer. No. There were people who wanted to take advantage but they were talked to. Now they no longer want to take advantage. One or two may have been encouraged to leave, but they were not killed."

"Well, that's good at least."

There were more questions I could ask, but I decided I didn't want to know the answers. Those marriage vows might come into play and I did not want to end up betraying one of my best friends in order to honor my marriage.

Instead I asked, "Did you know anything about Agnes Rockmorton?"

"No."

"Any idea how someone could come up with a bunch of money real fast? The kind you spend buying a boat and sailing around the Caribbean?"

There was a slight pause. "Mm. For me it was jewels that I sold, first those I stole then those I was given. Then it was a nice divorce settlement. Another divorce settlement. Another one. Another. Some investments I liquidated. And, of course, being widowed. If Luke were not planning on spending the money on a vacation there are, of course, those people who will loan money quickly and then perhaps kill if it does not come back, but that is not the case here, no? A man does not borrow from that type of person to go on a vacation."

"Anything else you can think of?"

"There is also inheriting money, no? Although Luke did not seem the type to have a rich relative. And there is gambling. Someone local did win the lottery. I do not know that the prize has been claimed. Could Luke have been the winner?"

"Maybe. I don't know. I'll have to ask around. See if he was one to buy tickets. Thank you, Greta."

"You are quite welcome. I will see you soon?"

"Yes, let's have lunch next week. Lord knows there's nothing else on my plate."

"Maggie, tell me, what have you done this week. Work-wise?"

I thought about it for a second. "Let's see…I rebranded our entire product line and updated the website with all the new images. And, of course, had to coordinate that with the drop shippers we use to make sure they had all the new files."

"And you designed these images yourself?"

"Yeah."

"This week?"

"Yes."

"Anything else?"

I wrinkled my nose trying to remember. "I came up with another dog treat, but I don't know what to call it yet."

"And meetings for the resort, no?"

"Well, of course. You were on a couple of them weren't you?"

"I was. So. To summarize. You redid all of the branding for your treat line. You then updated your entire website and made sure the drop shippers had the new files. You also designed a new dog treat and participated in a number of meetings related to the new resort."

I nodded. "Yeah, sounds about right."

"You also were investigating a murder at the same time."

"Yes."

"And yet you think you are bored and have done nothing all week?"

I shrugged even though she couldn't see it. "Well, I am bored."

"Maggie."

"What? I am."

"You may be bored. But you are not unproductive. You must think about this. You do quite a bit while bored."

"Hm. True. Never really thought about it that way before. It's just that I could be doing so much more..."

"Maggie. Enjoy this time while you have it. It will not last. One day you will have kids and then you will never be bored—or sleep—again."

I decided not to dive into that conversation. "Good point, Greta. Thank you."

"Of course. What are friends for."

We hung up and I stared at the wall, thinking. Had Luke won the lottery? Was that the source of his sudden, new-found wealth? But if so, what did Agnes Rockmorton have to do with it? So many questions, and still no answers.

CHAPTER 24

Normally I would've just given up and gone to bed at that point because with Fancy liking to be up so early I need to go to bed early to get my beauty rest. But I was on a roll and I figured it was still early enough to call Jamie.

"Hey, Maggie, how's it going?" she said, sounding slightly surprised to hear from me so late at night.

"Good. How about you?"

"Okay..."

"Jamie, things are never just okay with you? What's wrong?"

She paused and then said, "I may have just screamed at Mason because we didn't have any double chocolate chunk pretzel ice cream in the house. And I may have told him to go to the store and find some or find somewhere else to sleep tonight."

"Jamie!"

"I know. I should call him and tell him to come back. But I really want that double chocolate chunk pretzel ice cream."

I managed not to laugh as I answered, "I've never seen that kind of ice cream at the store. Who makes it? I've long ago lost track of all the Ben & Jerry's flavors, is it one of theirs?"

Another pause. "Uhhh...Not that I'm aware of? As far as I know, no one makes it? But they should. Because it would be really good. With little chunks of chocolate in there and then crunchy pretzels on a base of dark chocolate ice cream."

"It certainly sounds good. Maybe we can have a line of homemade ice creams at the resort and that can be one of the flavors," I suggested.

"Oh, that's brilliant." I could hear her smiling through the phone. "I'm almost done experimenting with baby foods. Do you know how boring baby food is? Because you're not supposed to put things in it, like salt and sugar. It's just plain fruits and vegetables all mashed up. But ice cream...Now that I could have some fun with. I'm going to call Mason and tell him to pick me up some ingredients. And some samples from the store so I can see what works and what doesn't. But do we have enough room in the freezer...?"

I glanced at the clock. "Just remember that the store closes at ten, so you may have to put this off until tomorrow. No twenty-four hour grocery stores around here, what with wandering wildlife and all."

"Right."

There was another pause and then Jamie said, "Oh no, Maggie, what did I do?" Her voice started to tremble. "I sent Mason out **at night**. Do you know how dark the road can be between here and Masonville? And there are deer. What if he hits one? I mean he has a good vehicle, but what about the deer? And, oh Maggie, I can't handle it if he ends up in the hospital. What if I go into labor early?"

I tried not to laugh. "You're only like five or six months along, aren't you?"

"Exactly. I need him here. What was I thinking?" her voice spiraled as she talked until she was practically squeaking out the last word.

"Jamie," I said, using my parental command voice.

"Yes?"

"I want you to breathe with me, okay?" I continued, keeping my voice level and calm.

"Okay," she said quietly.

"Ready? In...."

I heard her take a deep breath on the other end of the line.

"And out..."

She exhaled slowly.

"And in..."

"Maggie, I can't be breathing right now when Mason is out there possibly running over a deer and I'm at home all alone with no one to help if I go into labor." The words tumbled out so fast I could barely understand her.

Once more I tried not to laugh because I knew she meant what she was saying no matter how absurd it actually was. "Remember those hormones we were talking about?" I asked. "I think they're kicking your butt right now."

"I...Oh. Maybe." She seemed to deflate.

"You okay now?" I asked, letting a hint of amusement finally show.

"I guess. I'd still like Mason to come home. I should call him."

She sounded like she was about to hang up on me, so I interrupted. "Real quick before you go?"

"Yeah?"

"Did Luke ever buy a lottery ticket as long as you knew him?"

"No. He wasn't the type. His dad had a gambling addiction, so Luke never bet on anything, ever. Wouldn't even play penny slots." At last she sounded like her normal self, scarily competent.

"Can't blame him for that," I said. "Sure-fire way to lose money in my book. Unless it's the hundred-play poker machines."

She laughed. "But it's so fun with the little bonus rounds. There was this game I played once that had these cute little chickens that would hatch out of an egg. And another one that had those nesting Russian dolls and each one that opened up gave you coins. I love those games."

"As long as you're prepared to lose the money, I guess." I shrugged. "I don't like being at the mercy of a machine that's programmed to make more money than I do."

"Maggie, you're too serious sometimes. It's just fun. But I should go. Because I want to call Mason and tell him to come home right now."

"Okay. Talk to you later. And if you go into labor before he gets back, you can always call me."

"Good point. Thanks. Bye."

I hung up, shaking my head. Poor Mason. I wasn't his biggest fan, but the man was going to have earned sainthood by the end of this pregnancy.

CHAPTER 25

The next day I tried to forget about Luke and Agnes and just enjoy the mid-summer day that I was able to spend with Fancy. We sat out in the backyard after lunch, her taking a nap, me reading my latest book. I was glad we were still able to get packages into the valley (via helicopter) because I would've died without enough books to read. I'd been consuming them at an unholy rate all year.

Reading is my stress relief. The worse things get, the more I read. I remember one year in college I was working full-time and had five finals in seven days and I somehow managed to read three books that week. (And also miraculously did not fail any of those finals although I do think one of those classes was the one where I got a C+ which thoroughly shocked and horrified me. I was always an A- student which meant sometimes a B or B+ student, but I was never a C student for crying out loud.)

Anyway. I was trying to distract myself with reading. But the book was…not that good. I hate to say that about a book, but it just really wasn't doing it for me. And I didn't have anything else to read because I am still an old-school reader who likes physical books so I couldn't just go online and replace it with something more engaging without having to wait an unknown number of days for it to be delivered.

Which meant my mind started to wander. And when my mind started to wander it landed right back on the murders of Lucas Dean and Agnes Rockmorton.

I was at a dead-end. And I hated that. I didn't want to quit. I didn't want to leave it up to Matt and his colleagues to figure out. I'd solved a number of murders already, there was no reason I shouldn't be able to solve these, too.

I just had to figure out where Luke thought he was going to get money from. If I could figure that out, I'd know who had killed him and Agnes and why.

Unfortunately, the only person capable of telling me that was probably Johnny Duffy. And I had no idea where to find him. Even if I did, he could be the killer so maybe it wasn't the smartest idea to go tracking him down to ask questions.

I was glaring at the book that had failed to capture my attention and contemplating asking around to find out where Johnny Duffy lived when a firework went off next door in Lucas Dean's backyard.

As Fancy jumped to her feet and ran around barking her displeasure, I raced to the fence and jumped up on the little board that ran along the bottom so I could see over the top. I smiled. It was Johnny Duffy. Just the man I wanted to see.

Before he could notice me and run away again, I dashed out the front gate and barged around the side of Luke's house to where an old white pickup with rust over the wheel wells was parked at an angle. The back of the truck already had about a dozen boxes of fireworks loaded up, and as I came around the driver's side Johnny Duffy came out of the back gate of Luke's house lugging another couple of boxes.

"Stop right there," I said.

He ignored me until he'd set the boxes down in the back of the truck and then turned to glare at me, wiping his nose on his forearm like the class act he was.

I placed myself between him and the driver's-side door. "I have some questions to ask you."

"Well I don't wanna answer no questions, so tough." He started to walk past me.

"I'll call the cops."

He stopped, close enough he could grab me if he wanted. "Why would you do that?"

"Because you're stealing from a dead man."

He stepped closer, glaring at me. "I'm not stealing. Luke and I bought these together. He's clearly not going to use them now."

Aleksa Baxter

I lifted my chin, holding my ground. "How do I know you're telling the truth? If you bought them together why were they at Luke's house?"

"Because he had the party. But we didn't use them all because he said his little busybody neighbor would probably call the cops if we set too many off after she got back home." He leaned in as he spoke, close enough for me to get a whiff of his tobacco breath.

I nodded. "He was probably right. My husband is a cop after all."

"Big whoop. These fireworks are mine and I'm going to take 'em." He started to walk away.

"Is that all you're taking?" I made a point of peering at the boxes in the truck.

He turned back. "Yeah."

"Why'd you wait so long?"

He spit to the side. "Like you said, they were in a dead man's house. Figured I'd wait a bit in case the cops needed to look through them."

I was honestly glad to see the fireworks go, so really didn't want to stop him from taking them. But I did

178

still need to know if Johnny Duffy had any clues about the murder.

"I'll make you a deal," I said. "I won't call the cops about this if you answer a few questions for me."

He shook his head. "Fine. But let's do this inside. They're mine, but no need to have anyone else come along and start asking a bunch of questions."

"Okay. Lead the way."

He pulled a tarp across the back of the truck before leading me into the house.

(I know. It was stupid to walk into a house no one knew I was at with a man who could possibly be the killer. But, one, I'm not always the brightest bulb. And, two, I really didn't think Johnny Duffy was the killer. A man in need of a good makeover, sure. A killer? Eh. Nah. **Probably** not.)

CHAPTER 26

Based on what I'd previously seen of his backyard, I was surprised that Luke's kitchen was as tidy as it was until I remembered that he'd hosted a party at his house the night he was killed. He must've cleared everything out of the downstairs, which meant that if there was anything interesting to see it would be upstairs.

I immediately headed in that direction while Johnny Duffy shouted at me to come back and stay in the kitchen.

"I'm not that kind of girl, thanks," I said as I headed up the creaky staircase by the front door.

"I didn't say you could go barging through his house. I thought you wanted to ask me questions." He followed me up the stairs, his heavier weight making each step sigh instead of creak.

"I do. But I also want to see if Luke had some sort of office where there might be a clue to where the money he was coming into was coming from."

"What are you talking about?" He caught up to me as I reached the narrow hallway. On the left was a bedroom that was much more typical of how I usually thought of Luke. There were clothes thrown all over the place and the bed wasn't made.

(Not that I ever make my bed either. Why should I when no one else will see it and it's just going to be slept in again that night? Of course, with Matt around now the bed is usually made because he gets up after me and is definitely one to tidy his environment.)

I turned to the room across the hallway. It was a small bathroom with a sink that could use a good wipe down. How can a man shave all the hair off his face and not bother to look down to see that half of it is now in the sink?

I kept going down the hall. The next room on the bathroom side was an office. Clearly everything that had been downstairs had been tossed into it because there were newspapers on the floor with a greasy metal something or other that looked half-assembled as well as random cans of paint and an automatic drill scattered across the floor along with at least three stacks of papers on the desk.

I noted the location of the drill as Johnny Duffy followed me into the room. Never hurts to know where a weapon is, just in case. I wrinkled my nose because he was close enough behind me I could smell the sour scent of him.

"What money?" he asked.

"So Luke didn't mention it to you? That he was coming into some money?" I glanced through the first pile of papers as we talked.

"No."

I turned to study him. "I thought he might've found something at Agnes's house."

"No." He truly looked bewildered by my questions. Clearly that was a dead end.

"Then why'd you get all weird and leave the grocery store the other day?" I asked, leaning against the desk.

He looked away from me, visibly uncomfortable. "Do you know what that place was like before we cleared it out? I didn't want to think about it, let alone talk about it in public."

I was dying to know what it had looked like, but I stayed focused. "Was it weird enough to blackmail someone over?"

"Blackmail? That old bat was proud of it. Tried telling us stories about the parties she'd had down there." He shook himself. "No. Nothing to blackmail her over. Just images I can't bleach out of my mind."

I raised my eyebrows, impressed by his use of imagery. I didn't think he had it in him. "So Luke didn't say anything to you about sailing the Caribbean this winter?"

"Oh, yeah, he couldn't stop talking about that the last week or so."

"How did you think he was going to pay for that?"

He blinked slowly. "I didn't give it much thought. Just figured he had the money."

"Someone said he was going to buy a boat."

He nodded. "That was part of the plan. Even showed me a picture of it. Probably somewhere here on his desk. Give me a minute."

He pawed through a large stack of papers on the corner of the desk. "Here it is. See? Nice looking, ain't it?"

I grabbed the rest of the papers that had been near the photo and glanced through them. "I'd say."

I showed him a print-out that said the boat cost seventy-five grand, new. Below that was a list of expenses for living in the Caribbean. Luke had been planning on a cost of three thousand a month for six months. So about a hundred grand total all told, maybe a little less.

I frowned at the calculations jotted down on that piece of paper. I thought he'd said it was life-changing money. I mean, don't get me wrong, someone wants to give me a hundred grand, I'll take it and do very nice things with it. And, yes, it would drastically improve my life or the life of most people. But when I think about life-changing money I think a million or more. Because that's enough to put in a bank account and invest and live off the interest. Less than that is just money to tidy things up with and maybe have a bit of fun.

Again, not that I wouldn't happily take any amount of money someone wanted to give me. But he'd said life-changing.

Maybe for Luke it was?

I grabbed the rest of the papers and thumbed through them. On one of the pages there was another series of jotted down numbers. One point five million and then an arrow to a value of seven hundred and fifty thousand. That was more like it.

Below the seven hundred and fifty thousand he'd written his current mortgage balance, what he owed on his truck, the hundred grand for six months in the Caribbean, and then some calculations about investing the rest, which would've been about four hundred thousand. It wasn't quite enough to quit his job long-term but it was enough to ease things certainly, especially with no mortgage or truck payment. With all of that it looked like he could have comfortably split his time between Colorado and the Caribbean and only worked half the year.

But the question still remained: where was the one point five million coming from? And who was he splitting it with?

I snapped a few pictures with my phone and then said, "Thanks" to Johnny Duffy and started back down the stairs.

"Wait. Where are you going? What's going on? What did you find out?" He stomped after me down the hall.

He'd seen the same things I had. Did I really have to spell it out for him? I shook my head as I made my way down the stairs, but stopped in the living room to explain it to him. "From those papers it's pretty clear Luke was coming into about seven hundred and fifty grand. Splitting half of one point five million. But I still don't know where that was coming from."

"The lottery."

When I didn't say anything he added, "It was on the news. Cash payout for whoever won the lottery the week before Luke died was going to be just about one point five million. I remember because I tried to figure out what that would look like in twenty-dollar bills. Like if it was enough to swim in or whatever."

I curled my lip at the thought. "You'd want to swim in money? Have you ever had a job where you handled money before? Because that stuff is nasty dirty. I used to run a cashier's office and by the end of the night my hands were literally black with crud from all those bills."

He hunched his shoulders. "I would've ordered it direct from the bank."

"You would've had to order it direct from the mint."

Before I could get distracted wondering if the mint actually printed currency bills as well as coins, I grabbed my phone and looked up the

Colorado Lottery website. Sure enough. The big winner that had been on the news and was still unclaimed had a cash payout value just under one point five million.

I shook my head. "I don't get it. Jamie told me Luke never played the lottery. She said his dad was a degenerate gambler so he never touched any of that."

"Yeah, that's true."

"So how did he end up with half of a winning ticket?"

"And where is it now?"

It was my turn to blink slowly. "Right. Good point. Whoever has the ticket is likely to be the killer."

"Huh? How's that?" Johnny looked at me, clearly confused by my leap of logic.

"Well, it makes sense, right? Why kill Luke if it wasn't for the ticket?"

"But whoever killed Luke also killed that old bat. Why kill her?"

I smiled. "I bet she was the other half. He must've picked the ticket up for her and they agreed to split the money fifty-fifty and then they won.

Whoever killed both of them found out about it and wanted the money all for themselves."

He shook his head. "Don't know about all that."

I looked at the corner of the living room where there was still a blood stain on the carpet. "You ever have military training?"

"Nah."

"You know anyone around here who did?"

He grunted. "Lots of guys. Especially the older ones. Most served. You think whoever killed Luke was military?"

"Not exactly common to stab someone in the kidney."

He crossed his arms and rocked back on his heels. "Huh. Never thought much about it. Won't help you, though. Too many guys around here like that. Plus you got the hunters. All of them know their way around a knife."

"Fair point." I headed towards the kitchen. "Well, thank you. Appreciate the time."

Aleksa Baxter

We walked back outside and I winced as the late afternoon sun hit me in the eyes.

"My pleasure." He smiled at me in a way that was almost friendly as Fancy started barking from the other side of the fence.

She couldn't see us, but clearly she'd heard us. "Hush, Fancy. I'll be there in just a minute."

I wanted to immediately go over to Patrice Cole's house and ask her to let me into Agnes Rockmorton's so I could look for signs of the lottery ticket to confirm my newest theory, but it was Fancy's dinnertime and one thing I had learned over the years was that it wasn't wise to delay her dinner.

(Not that Fancy would be destructive or even difficult about it, she'd just give me the saddest, most hurt look in the world, and I'd do pretty much anything to keep that look out of her eyes.)

So home it was. And then...Find the killer.

CHAPTER 27

I was all ready to solve the murder now that I knew where Luke was probably getting the money, but when I really sat down and started to think it through I was still as stuck as I had been before. The "Luke and Agnes buy a lottery ticket" theory was good, but the problem was who else would've known about the ticket? And why kill Luke before they killed Agnes?

It didn't make sense. There was still something I had to be missing. But what?

I tried to do research on who might know how to knife a person in the kidneys, but all that did was lead me down some disturbing internet rabbit holes I would've rather avoided. So, as much as I was sure my grandpa was sick of my doing so, I took myself and Fancy over to his house and invited myself to dinner.

Lesley had made an absolutely delicious lasagna. (And I can assure you that I had more than one fist-sized serving's worth, thank you very much.)

Since my grandpa doesn't believe in talking business during dinner we talked about the fundraiser instead.

"It's too bad Agnes won't be there this year," Lesley said.

"Why's that?" I asked.

"Because she was always the biggest buyer of pickles. Her and Jolene Paige. Between the two of them they'd buy up half our supply every event."

"You're talking about those peel open things you can get that look like a slot machine when you open them up?"

"Yes, pickles."

"I once won twenty bucks on one of those at a little Italian festival in Denver. I think I was like ten. It was probably illegal for me to be playing but no one seemed to mind. So

Jolene **and** Agnes bought them? Together?" I asked, taking another bite of yummy pasta, sauce, and cheese.

"Oh yes. They'd pool their money, spend about a hundred dollars each time, and then stake out a table in the corner and go to work."

Lesley took a much more modest bite of her lasagna as I asked, "Did they ever make money off of it? That's a lot to spend if you're not going to get it back."

She nodded as she thought about it. "Yes. I'm pretty sure they did. They also used to go in on buying a lottery ticket each week. Had their lucky numbers that they just swore would win them the jackpot one day."

"You said used to?" I asked, leaning in, sensing a vital clue had just been uncovered.

"Maggie May," my grandpa interrupted. "It's dinner. No murder at the dinner table."

"But we're not talking murder, we're talking lottery tickets."

He didn't say anything, just gave me a look until I turned my attention back to finishing up my last little bit of garlic bread. (Homemade under the broiler and oh so good.)

Only after I'd let Fancy lick the plate clean of pasta sauce and helped load all the dishes into the dishwasher, did I bring the conversation back to those lottery tickets. "So, Lesley. About those lottery tickets that Jolene and Agnes used to buy together. Did they always play the same numbers?"

"Of course. It was some combination of their birthdays and their husbands' birthdays. They played them for years but never won."

"Any chance you know Agnes's birthday?"

My grandpa handed me a small journal with my grandma's handwriting scrawled on the pages. "Probably in here. Marie knew everyone's birthday."

I flipped through the pages. It was a birthday journal with a set of pages for every month. Each day of the month was listed on a separate line with names scrawled on the line for whoever's birthday was on that given day. I blinked back my tears as I scanned the names written in my grandma's once-familiar handwriting.

I missed her.

But there was a murderer to catch, so I kept going. I found Agnes on March 21st and Theodore on August 15th. That gave me 3-21-8-15.

I grabbed my phone and pulled up the winning lottery numbers for the ticket I suspected Luke and Agnes had bought.

Sure enough, 3-8-11-15-21-30. All four of the numbers were included, which made it likely that Jolene or Charles Paige had a birthday on the 30th and either a birthday on the 11th or in November. I flipped through the book, but didn't find entries for either one.

"Why did they stop playing the numbers together?" I asked, waiting for everything to finish clicking into place.

"I don't know. They'd been a little cold towards one another the last year or so. Might be politics."

"Do you know if either one continued to play those numbers?"

She shook her head. "I don't. Sorry."

I tried not to think about murder for the rest of the night as my grandpa, Lesley, and I played a few games of Scrabble. (I lost. My grandpa is a word-shark and Lesley was far too good at catching even the slightest mistake. Leave one triple-word-score open...) But it was hard. I was so close, but something just wasn't falling into place.

CHAPTER 28

I made it home just before Matt. He looked awful as he came through the door wearing a t-shirt and sweats instead of his uniform. (Not that Matt can ever truly look awful, but he looked like he'd been run through the wringer a few times.)

"Bad day at work?" I asked, dying to talk to him about what I'd found, but trying to be a good, dutiful wife.

"The worst. Give me a second to get a load of laundry started."

"I can do it," I half-heartedly offered while secretly hoping he wouldn't take me up on it.

"No. You really don't want to."

Whatever was going on with the clothes he had in the bag, Fancy was definitely interested. She trotted along next to him, sniffing away, clearly wanting to tear the bag right out of his hands.

As he passed closer, I retreated into the kitchen. "What is that smell?"

Matt didn't answer until he'd thrown his uniform into the washing machine and turned it on. "Do we have beer?" he joined me in the kitchen.

I handed him one and he took a big long swallow and then closed his eyes and just stood there swaying on his feet for a moment.

Noticing that his hair was wet, I asked, "Did you take a shower at work?"

He nodded. "A quick one. At Ben's."

"Why not come home?"

"Because we were only a few blocks from Ben's house when this happened. His wife actually offered to wash my uniform, too, but I didn't want to make her deal with it what with the new baby and all."

"So what happened?" I asked.

"Failed overdose. No good deed goes unpunished. The person we went to help lost their cookies all over me, hence the shower and change of clothes."

"Will they be okay?" I started to heat him up the leftover lasagna for dinner.

"I hope. They seemed stable by the time the ambulance pulled away."

"Who was it?"

He took another long swig of his beer. "Can't tell you. HIPAA rules."

I tried not to roll my eyes, but I probably failed. I knew if it was me I'd want someone to respect my privacy and not go talking about my drug issues all over town, but still. I was his wife and I liked to have a face to put to things.

Ah well. A failed drug overdose wasn't my concern. Murder was.

"I had a break in the case today," I told him as the microwave beeped and I put his plate on the table. (A serving which was most certainly larger than the size of Matt's fist. Heck, the garlic bread that went with it was larger than the size of Matt's fist.)

When I saw him glance towards the microwave with a slight wince I went back and wiped down the splattered sauce on the inside. (I tell ya, marriage has so many little potholes you can step in.)

"The case? And what case would that be?" He crossed his arms and stared me down.

I pressed my lips together and narrowed my eyes as I looked back at him. He didn't sound happy. Why? What was wrong?

This living with someone thing was weird. Because you were around them all the time, even when they were in a cranky mood and maybe didn't want to be bothered with you.

See, when you're dating—especially when it hasn't been all that long which was the case with Matt and I before we got married—you can manage to only see the person when you're in the mood to see them and they're in the mood to see you.

But get married and suddenly you're spending time together when you're exhausted or cranky or sad or just not in a mood to people. And, sure, for some people that's why they get married—to have someone who will be there for them when they're all those things. But for me...

Well, it was a little hard to realize that sometimes Matt didn't want to hear about something that really mattered to me in that moment because he needed me to listen to him instead.

It seems I'm not good at coddling. But I was willing to try.

I shook my head. "Never mind. Drink your beer, eat your lasagna, get a nice night's sleep, and we'll talk about it in the morning."

"Maggie," he sighed. "Just tell me now."

I winced. "Are you sure? You've had a long day."

"Positive."

He didn't sound positive. He sounded like a parent about to find out his kid had wrecked the car. But he'd asked, so...

As he ate his lasagna I told him about my venture to Luke's house that afternoon and then about what Lesley had told me about Jolene Paige and Agnes Rockmorton buying a lottery ticket together all those years.

When I was done I added, "So see? Luke must've bought a lottery ticket for Agnes and she must've told him they could split it. But Jolene Paige was upset because she'd helped choose and play those numbers all those years, so she must've had them killed so she could take the money instead."

He took another bite of lasagna before saying anything. "You've met Jolene Paige. Did she strike you as a double-murderer?"

"No. But who else could've known about the lottery ticket?"

He rubbed his fingers through his hair and sighed. "I don't know, Maggie. But I don't think it was Jolene Paige. Why would Luke even let her in the door at his party? **After** everything was over? And if there was some sort of rift between Jolene and Agnes, why would Agnes let her in? If the murders had occurred in the opposite order, maybe I'd believe it was Jolene. Maybe. But Luke was first."

I slumped down in my chair. "You're right. So we're looking for someone who knew Luke well enough to be at his party or to go back to his house after the party, and for him to open the door and let them in. And he wasn't wearing his shirt, so it must've been someone who came back. Or who stayed and started something that involved losing bits of clothing...Hm. Not Jolene Paige territory, is it?"

"Nope."

"But the lottery ticket angle could still be valid. Whoever redeems that ticket, you have to check into them. They were almost certainly playing Agnes and Jolene's numbers."

"I'm pretty sure winners can use a corporate shell to protect their identities when they claim their winnings. If that's the case, I'd have to have some very good evidence to pierce that."

I glanced at the fridge. I wanted a drink. But it was too late for me to get started. My days of drinking until two and sleeping until noon had long since passed me by.

Aleksa Baxter

I frowned at the table. "Darn it. So I'm back at square one."

Matt finished off his beer. "**You** are not anywhere, because **this** is not your case. But if it were, you're not at square one. We know that Luke had likely purchased that lottery ticket or was splitting it fifty-fifty with whoever had purchased it. And we know that Agnes very likely played those exact numbers every week for years. So the lottery ticket is key to finding the killer. We just don't know who that would be."

"Do you have a list of who was at the party?"

He looked at me, exhaustion in every line of his body. "Maggie. Not your case."

"I promise I'll give you a really good back massage if you let me see the list of who was at the party."

"Oh good, now my wife is bribing me with sexual favors."

"First, a back massage is not sex. Just like dancing is not sex. People seem to confuse those things often."

"If it's really good it leads to it." He winked at me and grinned.

"Matthew Allen Barnes. Clean up your mind. Second, I'll give you the massage either way because you look like you need it. But I figured it was worth a try to see if I could leverage it to get the list from you. So it's not bribery. It's just...subterfuge."

"Subterfuge?" He smiled and raised one eyebrow.

"Mmhm."

"Well, let's take you, your **subterfuge**, and that promised massage to the bedroom and we'll see what happens with that list come the morning."

I kissed him on the cheek as he laced his fingers in mine. "I love you, you know that?"

"Is that more subterfuge?"

"Oh stop using that word. And, no, it is not. I love you. Pure and simple. No subterfuge about it."

He laughed and pulled on our joined hands. "Well, for what's it's worth, I love you, too. Even if you do keep butting your nose into my cases."

CHAPTER 29

The next afternoon Matt let me tag along to the police station so he could give me the list of everyone who'd been at the party.

"Come on," he said after grabbing the list off his desk. "We'll go sit in the interview room. More space there."

I held back. "Do we have to? It's not exactly my favorite room. We could just go back home."

"Maggie, I'm on duty."

"But it's a block away. If something comes up, they can page you or whatever. Call on the radio. Call your cellphone. Marlene won't mind, will you, Marlene?" I asked the kindly woman at the reception desk.

"Not at all, dear."

"See?"

Matt shook his head. "I have to maintain a professional appearance, Maggie. And solving a murder case at my kitchen table does not do that."

"Don't be silly. Because solving the murder case, period, is far more important than where you're sitting or what you're wearing while you do so."

He shook his head again, crossed his arms, and planted his feet. "No. If you want the list, we look at it in the interview room."

I huffed out an exasperated breath, but I knew that stubborn set to his jaw. He wasn't going to back down on this one. "Fine. Let's go to the interview room."

As we started down the hall, Officer Clark walked through the front door.

"Ben," Matt called, "we're going to go over some evidence in the Dean and Rockmorton murders. You want to join us?"

He looked at me and then Matt, but didn't comment on who the "we" Matt was referring to was. "Sure. Let me get some coffee and I'll be right in."

Aleksa Baxter

Once Officer Clark joined us, I explained what I'd learned from Luke's house and from Lesley.

Officer Clark leaned forward and fixed me with a glare. "So you admit Ms. Carver that you were trespassing in the home of a dead man and that you took his property?"

"No. I admit no such thing. I was granted entry to the home of a dead man by a man who told me he had lawful access to that home. And I did not take any documents from the house, I took photos of those documents. Plus, aren't we here to solve the case not arrest our co-worker's wife for...whatever?"

"Meddling."

"I'm not..." I shook my head. "Look. Things just fall into my lap sometimes, alright? And it is my civic duty to share those things with you so that you can find the killer. What kind of member of society would I be if I knew about Luke's lottery win, or potential lottery win, and didn't share that with you? Or about the connection between Agnes and Jolene and didn't share **that** with you?"

"And you being here right now?" he asked.

"I can't know what's important to share with you if I don't have adequate information. The more I know, the more I can tell you what I've stumbled across that's helpful to you. That's all."

He looked at Matt who shrugged and said, "She has been helpful."

He shook his head. "One of these days she's going to get herself into trouble she can't get out of."

I waved my hand in the air. "Excuse me. Right here. In the room. No need to talk about me like I'm not here."

Officer Clark turned his steely gaze on me. "One of these days you are going to get yourself into trouble you can't get out of. You will be alone with someone, like Johnny Duffy, and he'll turn out to be the actual killer and he will kill you. Walk your dog, knit something, read a book, I don't care. But stay out of murder cases."

I crossed my arms and slouched down in my chair, feeling like a bratty twelve-year-old. "It happened right next door to me. I didn't go looking for it."

"You're from DC, right? That's where you were living before this?"

"Yes."

"And if someone next door had been killed in DC, would you have gone investigating it?" He leaned forward like this was an actual interrogation.

"No. You crazy? I had a friend who lived a block from a triple murder but no way if that had been me would I have ever asked questions. I would've been shot."

"And yet here you are."

"But here I know people. I'm part of the community. It's not some stranger killing a stranger over something like drugs that has nothing to do with me. It's someone I might know killing someone I'd known for years. It's different."

He shook his head. "No, it's not. A killer is still a killer. And once someone has killed for the first time it's easier to do it again."

I wanted to ask if he knew that from personal experience because

I'm a smart aleck that way, but I didn't. "I promise as long as it isn't my neighbor or someone I directly know and love that is either the victim or the suspect, that I will not investigate any more murders. But for now, I'm investigating this one. And I can do so here safely with you guys, or I can go poking around on my own. Your call."

Officer Clark looked at Matt. "I can't believe you married this woman."

"She keeps me on my toes. And I like her dog." He winked at me before I could pretend to be outraged. Quite frankly, I couldn't believe he'd married me either.

"So? The case? Who was at the party?" I asked.

CHAPTER 30

Matt started reading from a list of attendees that turned out to be three pages long. It seemed half the frickin' county had been at Luke's party at some point. That didn't help.

I asked, "Do you have any times on those people? When they arrived, when they left?"

Matt shook his head. "We tried, but people were fairly vague so I'm not sure it helps."

He slid the list across the table to me and I read through it again. "Anyone on here related to Jolene Paige? A son, daughter, grandson, granddaughter?"

Both Matt and Officer Clark shook their heads.

"Okay….What about…Who on this list is a woman who is attractive enough that Luke would open the door if she came back after the party, and who might also have enough experience with a knife to know how to knife someone in the kidney?"

Matt nodded. "That's a good angle. Let's see." He took the list back from me and he and Officer Clark debated over it, marking the names with little stars for the attractive women and little exes for the ones that probably knew how to use a knife. At one point Officer Clark left the room to ask Marlene about the names, because neither he nor Matt could remember what a few of the women looked like.

They were then able to eliminate most of the names because they had alibis for one or both of the murders which left us with two names: Trinity Jessup and Nicole Grant.

"Those sound familiar," I said. "I think both of their grandmothers were at that Ladies' Auxiliary meeting. Which means they're very likely going to be at the library fundraiser."

Matt, because he knew me too well, said, "Maggie."

"What? Are you telling me they're suspect enough that you can bring them in right now?"

Matt and Officer Clark looked at each other and both shook their heads.

"So let me do what I do best, which is pry information out of people I barely know."

Matt laughed. "Is that what you do best?"

"Matthew Allen Barnes, don't start with me."

Officer Clark leaned back in his chair and muttered, "Still don't see why you married her..."

"I am right here," I snapped. "And for the record, I've met your wife and I don't know how such a sweet, adorable woman found you to be all that. So pot, kettle, back off." I turned my attention to Matt. "Now, do you guys want my help or not?"

"Do we have a choice?" he asked.

"You could solve the murder before the event tomorrow. Then I'd have no reason to try to chat these ladies up."

"Maggie. Be nice."

"Sorry. I was just stating facts. If you solve the murder before tomorrow then there's no reason for me to talk to them. But if it's still open then I will feel compelled to do what I can to close the loop. Because if it doesn't get closed I will be thinking about these stupid murders somewhere in the back of my mind for the rest of my frickin' life. And I don't know about you, Officer Barnes, but I'd rather not have Lucas Dean and his short shorts lurking in the back of my mind for the next fifty years."

"If you put it that way. But I should be there with you. Just in case."

"Oh, hadn't I told you? You were already going to be there. I signed you up for the dunk tank."

"The dunk tank." He didn't sound excited by that possibility.

I shrugged. "They decided not to have a kissing booth this year. Not to mention, had someone actually tried to kiss you I might've had an issue with that, even if it was for charity."

"So instead you signed me up to be dunked in water."

"Well, it has been a year for unhappiness with cops. We figured it might be a big money-earner. And I knew you'd step up and do your part for the library. For Lesley. For my grandpa. And for me."

"Maggie May."

I turned to Officer Clark. "Of course, if Officer Clark here would like to volunteer in your stead..."

"If I volunteer your grandpa will probably throw his arm out trying to dunk me."

"Exactly. Think of all the money that will make for the library." I smiled and batted my eyes at him before glancing away so Matt could silently beg Officer Clark to take his place without losing face with me.

After a moment or two, Officer Clark grunted. "Fine. I'll do it. I'll sit in the dunk tank so Matt can help you interview our potential suspects."

"Thank you," I said, sincerely. "You know, I'm starting to think you're not so bad after all."

He didn't say anything, just glared at me.

"Well, better get going." I flashed both Matt and Officer Clark a grin, lingering on Officer Clark as I added, "I do have a coffee cake to make for the bake sale portion after all. Us married ladies have to keep ourselves busy somehow. Don't want to poke our noses into men's business after all."

(That part was not so sincere.)

Matt stood to escort me outside. "I'd suggest you don't eat a slice if she says she made you one special." He patted Officer Clark on the shoulder before opening the door for me.

As we walked down the hall, I said, "Hey, now. Just because I was slightly miffed that he seemed to imply I should stay home like a good little housewife, does not mean I would bake him a cake with laxatives in it."

"But you thought about it."

"For a second. Maybe two. But I'd never do it."

He kissed my forehead as we stopped outside the entrance. "It's a good thing there are no actual thought police in this world, Maggie, or I'd have to arrest you once a week for attempted murder."

"Once a week? Try once a day. Try once an hour if I drift too close to Twitter. Or the news. Ugh."

He chuckled and pulled me close. "I am so glad I found you."

"So am I. Because you would've been able to find some cute little Suzie Homemaker with a perky ponytail who bounced when she walked and never said a mean word to anyone, but I would've ended up a lonely spinster if I'd never met you."

I gave him a quick kiss and headed home. Fancy was not going to be amused that I'd left her alone even if it had been for just an hour.

CHAPTER 31

The coffee cake did not go to plan. That's because I was using the recipe off my mom's old Bisquick can and I somehow started making pancakes instead of coffee cake. Don't ask me how I made that mix up, but fortunately I noticed my error before I added any of the wet ingredients. So I was able to sort of scoop out the excess ingredients that didn't belong in a coffee cake and add in the ones that did.

Surprisingly, it turned out tasty enough that three different people asked me for the recipe at the bake sale. Unfortunately, "start making pancakes and transform it into a coffee cake when you realize you've messed up" is not a recipe most people can follow easily, so instead I just played coy and told them it was an old family recipe I couldn't share.

Matt, who knew the truth, gave me a look the first time I said that, but I ignored him. In a sense it **was** an old family recipe—my mom used to make us coffee cake sometimes in the winter for dessert using that very recipe—and I also couldn't share it because I had no clue what I'd actually done to create that particular coffee cake.

I wasn't lying, I just wasn't telling them the full truth. What was so wrong about that?

After the coffee cake discussions I decided it was time to get down to business, but I wasn't sure where to find Trinity Jessup or Nicole Grant.

Fortunately, I knew exactly who to ask: Patrice Cole and Jolene Paige were clustered together in the corner exchanging whispered comments as they picked at their tiny little plates of food. If anyone knew the scoop, it would be them.

"Patrice. Jolene. How are you?" I asked, dragging Matt along with me. "Have you met my husband, Matt?"

Patrice answered for both of them. "I don't believe I ever have. Officer Barnes, a pleasure."

She extended her scarecrow hand in his direction and Matt took it and bowed slightly. "The pleasure is all mine."

(I'd warned him in advance not to say anything about my impromptu tour of Agnes Rockmorton's house. He was as good as his word, chatting casually about the fundraiser and how he was glad to not be in the dunk tank after all.)

Just as he said that we heard a loud splash and I looked over to see my grandpa grinning wickedly as he watched Officer Clark flounder around trying to get himself back on the little dunk platform.

"Aww, look at that. Grandpa's having fun," I said.

Jolene leaned close. "Does he have something against Officer Clark? That's the third time he's dunked him."

"Come now, Jolene. Don't tell me you don't know the full details behind the murder of Jack Dunner? You are far too informed a woman for me to believe that."

"Well, one does hear things. And I guess being arrested for a murder you didn't commit does tend to create some negative feelings, but I thought they'd moved past that."

"Mmm, maybe after today. Speaking of knowing things, tell me, do you know where I can find Trinity Jessup?"

"Trinity? She's right over there in the green dress. Lovely girl. And due any day now which is both exciting and scary in these times."

Sure enough, Trinity Jessup was sporting one very large baby bump. I figured I could rule her out as the killer. I mean, it wasn't **inconceivable** that a forty-weeks-pregnant woman could kill a man with a knife, but it was highly unlikely. Especially since we were assuming that whoever the killer was she'd gone back to Luke's after the party ended and he'd let her in expecting certain things to happen.

Luke was a sleaze, but I wasn't sure he was that much of a sleaze.

"Good for her," I said, mentally dropping her off my list.

"Speaking of babies," Patrice leaned in. "What about you two? You've been married a few months now. Are you pregnant yet?"

Just because we'd been married a few months did not mean we were going to start popping out kids like Tic Tacs. Although a disconcerting number of people seemed to think that's how it did or should work. And even if we were, that did not mean it was some random old woman's business. Didn't she realize that some people have trouble conceiving? And that maybe it's a little sensitive to ask about that sort of thing?

"You know," I answered, squeezing Matt's hand. "There's a lot of uncertainty going around these days, so we're taking our time with that."

"Dear, there's always uncertainty. There will never be a right time to have a kid, you just have to dive in there and do it. Like your friend Jamie did. Look at her. She's glowing with happiness."

And she was. This time in a bright pink dress that accented her adorable bump. I gave her a quick wave and turned back to the ladies, forcing myself to continue to smile and not run from the room.

There had actually been a point where I had this crazy notion that I might have a kid on my own and I'd floated the idea by a handful of mothers I knew. Literally every mother I spoke to with kids under the age of five told me not to do it, and every mother I spoke to with grown children told me it was absolutely worth doing no matter what.

Matt may have changed things—it's theoretically easier with two parents, assuming they're both equal participants—but not that much. Those mothers with young children I'd talked to had all been married and some of them had even had live-in help to go along with it and still there had a been a definite trend of "this will cost a few years of your life" in the answers they gave me.

(Two had even told me to never have kids. Ever.)

So, no. Not falling for that one just yet. And we were getting away from the point, which was to find Lucas Dean's killer.

"What about Nicole Grant? Is she here?"

"Nicole...She may be. I don't see her right now." Jolene craned her neck to look around the crowd.

"What does she look like?"

"You know. Average height. Brown hair. Oh, there she is. With her girlfriend. Who is a lovely woman it turns out despite the short hair."

I looked to where she'd pointed and saw two women standing together talking to a young man I also didn't recognize. One was a striking brunette with a gorgeous mane of hair, the other was an average-looking redheaded woman with her hair cut short above the ears.

"So Nicole is the one on the left with the longer hair then?"

"Yes. Exactly."

I pressed my lips together, trying to figure out how to ask the question I needed to ask without sounding like a horrible person. "You know, I believe

Nicole was at Lucas Dean's party the night he was killed. Was there ever anything between them?"

"You mean romantic?" Patrice asked with a titter. "Oh no. Nicole has always known what she liked and it was not...men. None of us were surprised when she returned from living in the city for a few years with her friend there. And those two are joined at the hip. If Nicole was at that party, Nat was too."

"Do you want me to introduce you?" Jolene asked.

"Oh no. That's fine. I'm sure I'll meet them later." I tried not to frown. Once more we were back at square one.

"Oh. Look who just waltzed in. Speaking of babies." Jolene nodded knowingly at Patrice.

"Such a surprise, wasn't it?" Patrice nodded back.

"What surprise was that?" I asked.

"Well, I hate to be a gossip," Jolene said, leaning in close. "But it was all quite sudden, wasn't it?"

"Most definitely," Patrice agreed.

"At least Carl stepped up and did the right thing."

"Mmhm," Patrice agreed again.

"Ladies? What are you talking about?" I asked.

Jolene placed her hand on my arm as she leaned in. "Addison West and Carl Rockmorton got married on Wednesday. Must be thirty years between them. He's just turned sixty and she can't be more than mid-30's. Didn't even know they were dating to be honest. And here suddenly they're married. And you just know what had to be behind that. Rushing to the altar. Only one reason to do that sort of thing."

I raised my eyebrows since I'd married Matt the day he proposed to me. "Not really."

"Of course, dear." She patted my hand. "Sometimes you just leave it all too late and can't wait out the niceties."

Matt, probably knowing that I was a step away from throttling her, put his arm around my shoulder and gave me a quick kiss on the cheek. "And sometimes you don't see the reason to wait on arbitrary timelines to start your forever with the woman you love. I know that was the case for me."

Both of the ladies gazed at him with slightly rapt expressions.

"Well, then," I said, taking the slim window of opportunity he'd presented. "We better get going. I think someone needs to stop my grandpa before he throws out his shoulder. Lovely talking to you."

"And you too, dear."

Somehow I managed to keep the fake smile on my face until I was far enough away to prevent anyone noticing the fire in my eyes.

CHAPTER 32

As we approached the dunk tank, my grandpa stood in front of it moving his shoulder around like it pained him.

"Honestly, Grandpa, enough. How many times have you dunked the man?"

"I lost count at five."

"Seven," Officer Clark called.

"You are going to need to ice that tonight and you'll be lucky if you aren't walking around with pain in that shoulder for the next week. Serves you right, really. You made your point, leave poor Officer Clark alone. Plus, we need him."

"You do?" Officer Clark asked from where he sat on the platform.

"We do. Come on. Let's give this a break."

My grandpa grumbled under his breath, but he let us lead Officer Clark off to the side.

Once the three of us were alone, Matt gave him a quick rundown on our suspects. And then added, "We learned something else interesting, though."

"What's that?" Officer Clark asked.

"Addison West and Carl Rockmorton got married on Wednesday. Unexpectedly. Maggie's friends thought it was because she was pregnant."

"But that can't be. Because..."

Matt nodded.

I looked back and forth between the two of them. "Does this have anything to do with you coming home in a pair of sweatpants the other night?"

He nodded again as all three of us looked over to where the young woman—an attractive blonde with ample curves—was hanging off of the arm of an older, slightly rumpled man. They were not an obvious couple.

"Is he rich?" I asked.

Officer Clark laughed. "No. But he is the only living child of Agnes Rockmorton and therefore likely to inherit everything she had—including perhaps a winning lottery ticket."

"So she's our killer, then," I said. "She found out about the lottery ticket, killed Luke so he wouldn't get half, then killed Agnes so that Carl would inherit the lottery winnings, and then seduced Carl into marrying her so she could get the money."

Matt scratched his chin as he thought about it. "That's a pretty elaborate way to earn yourself a million dollars."

"How else was she going to do it? Not like most people will see that kind of money in a lifetime. I figure opportunity presented itself and she struck."

"I don't know. It seems pretty convoluted to me. Why didn't she just take the ticket?"

"If it was already signed, she couldn't. And if Agnes Rockmorton turns up dead and then Addison West walks in with her lottery ticket—and not just random numbers, but ones Agnes played year in and year out—there'd be a lot of questions. But if Agnes Rockmorton dies and her son happens to find a winning lottery ticket in her house while going through her things, then it all seems reasonable. And if he happens to be married at that point, well then his wife shares in his good fortune and isn't she lucky."

Officer Clark frowned at them. "Why kill Luke?"

"So he couldn't tell on her? Plus, Luke had to die first so all the money would go to Agnes. I mean, maybe that wouldn't hold up in a court of law, but it's how I'd think about it in the moment. Two people have equal interests in the ticket but haven't cashed it in yet, one dies, their interest passes to the other."

Officer Clark and Matt looked at each other. "Worth a conversation," Officer Clark said.

Matt nodded. "Definitely. But we'll do it Monday. In the meantime..." He turned to me. "I think it's only fair that you take your turn in the dunk tank, too."

"Matt! You're my husband, you're supposed to protect me."

"It's for a good cause," he grinned at me, a wicked glint in his eye.

"But…"

"You volunteered me for it."

"Well, yes, but. **Matt**."

He just looked at me with those oh-so-blue eyes until I finally broke. "Fine. Fine, fine, fine. I will sit in the dunk tank. Probably nobody here that will even want to dunk me anyway."

Officer Clark laughed. "Are you kidding? I'm going to be first in line."

And he was. Followed by Jack and Mason and Johnny Duffy and a few other people I may have ruffled along the way. Even Jamie tried to dunk me!

Good news, most of them had horrible aim, but I did definitely take a dunking or two, which is how I managed to convince Matt that I had every right to be in the observation room when they interviewed Carl

Rockmorton and Addison West on Monday.

One thing I've learned about marriage: guilt can be a wonderful tool for getting what you want.

CHAPTER 33

I spent the rest of the weekend unable to sit still because Monday we were finally going to prove who had murdered Luke and Agnes and I couldn't wait.

(Yes, I realize that my excitement over solving the deaths of two human beings was probably not something anyone would consider healthy, but, hey, it takes all types. And if there weren't people like me who got excited about finding murderers, think how many more would go uncaught. Other people can get their thrills from watching football, I get my thrills out of solving things, in this case a double-murder.)

Of course, the reality of police work and the fantasy of police work are two entirely different things. And Carl

Rockmorton was, well, to put it politely, a very, very, very boring individual. He had pretty green eyes, I'll give him that, but it was like he had no emotional range at all. Every sentence was delivered in the exact same monotone voice.

There he was, talking about his new, attractive, much younger wife and he could've been talking about car parts for all the emotion he showed. (He owned a local store that carried a variety of automotive and machine parts.)

I won't force you to suffer through the experience of his entire interview. (Because quite frankly I don't want to suffer through describing it. Living it once was enough.) But the gist was that he'd unexpectedly met Addison West when she came into his shop looking for a new gas cap for her car. No one else was in the store so they'd started talking and she'd stuck around and one thing had led to another and they had dinner which led to other things which led to her suggesting that they should get married because why wait when things were so perfect.

And him, being an older, awkward man who'd written off ever meeting anyone, let alone a buxom younger woman, didn't see why not. Not like he had anything of value for her to take. And he figured why not get what he could while the getting was good. Stranger things had happened and he wasn't about to look at that particular gift horse too closely.

Upon further questioning it came out that they had met the day after Luke was killed, so before Agnes was killed.

That put an interesting twist on things until Matt pushed even more and found out that Carl had introduced Addison to his mother just two days later. And that they'd gone to Agnes's house for dinner and Carl had caught Addison in his mother's office when she'd said she was going to the restroom.

And then surprise, surprise, the next night someone had killed Agnes.

It wasn't too much of a stretch to think that Addison had initially slept with Carl to get access to his mother's house with the idea of just stealing the lottery ticket. But when

237

she found it, Agnes must have already signed it, so she had to go to Plan B.

Having already met Agnes, Addison must have gone back the next night with some flimsy excuse or the other and killed her. And then all that was left was to convince Carl to marry her before he found out about the lottery ticket.

It sounded good. Nice and plausible. A believable story about a younger woman manipulating an older, gullible man who didn't even know it had happened.

But something wasn't quite right with the way Carl told his story. It was subtle, but it was there. When Matt didn't quite ask the question that would bring out some critical little detail, Carl found a way to slip it in. It was like he had a mental checklist of things he needed the cops to hear and he couldn't bring himself to deviate from it.

I had a strong suspicion that Matt could wait two weeks, bring Carl back in for another round of questioning, and every single little detail would be the exact same. Because the story

Carl was telling was just that, a story. He wasn't remembering events, he was creating them.

Matt, because he's a brilliant, insightful man who is amazing at his job, (why no, I am not biased at all, thank you very much) knew it, too. Instead of ending the interview, he sat back in his chair and studied Carl for a long moment. And then he looked at the mirror where he knew I was and a small smile stretched his lips. Not enough of one to give things away to Carl, but enough of one to let me know that he'd seen it too.

"Well, thank you, Carl. I really appreciate it." He held out his hand and shook Carl's like they were just the best of friends now. "We'll talk to Addison next and then the two of you can be back on your way home. So sorry for the bother."

"My pleasure, Officer Barnes. Always happy to help." As Matt led him out the door I caught one quick glance of Carl Rockmorton's face as it was turned away and the smug little grin he allowed himself before returning to the bovine-like look he'd adopted for the cops.

CHAPTER 34

Just to be sure, before Matt started his interview with Addison I waved him into the observation room.

"You saw it, right? You know he's lying?" I asked.

He nodded. "But I'm not sure how to prove it."

"I have an idea. See, I think we were wrong about the timeline. We thought that Addison found out about the lottery ticket when she went to Luke's house that night. But Luke hadn't even told Trish and supposedly they were really, really close. So why would he tell Addison?"

"He wouldn't."

"Exactly. Luke was keeping it secret. But what if **Carl** told Addison? Before the party. What if she went to the party to find the lottery ticket not to kill Luke? What if killing Luke was just a mistake? Or unplanned?"

Matt rubbed his jaw thoughtfully. "So you're thinking Carl and Addison were working together before the party?"

I nodded.

"And that he sent her in to steal the lottery ticket?"

"Right. But she didn't find it. Or maybe she did. I don't know. But he's in on this somehow." I looked at Addison where she sat in the interview room, looking nervous, her perfectly-manicured nails drumming on the table.

Matt leaned against the window sill, studying her. "But there's no sign anyone else was there when Luke was killed other than the murderer. And I can't see him opening his door to Carl Rockmorton. Addison has to have been the one who killed Luke. We still don't know how she learned to stab someone in the kidney."

"I have an idea about that one. Jamie texted me this morning and asked if I would be up for taking self-defense classes after she has the baby. There's an ex-Army Ranger offering them and on his website he talks about kidney strikes." I showed him the website on my phone. "What if Addison took his class?"

"That would make sense. Okay. So I need to get her on the record that she took that self-defense class and learned about kidney strikes, and then I need her to admit she knew Carl before she went to that party at Luke's."

"What you really need is a confession."

He nodded. "I know. But all I can do is try to get what I can."

"If anyone can do it, you can." I gave him a quick kiss and pushed him towards the door, eager to see how he was going to pull it off. Because I knew he would.

(Yes, I do have an unwavering faith in my husband. Because he has earned it.)

CHAPTER 35

Matt started off friendly. "Addison, thank you so much for coming to see me today. I hate to bring you in here like this, but you have to understand that we need to cross all those t's and dot all those i's. And since you did just suddenly marry the man who's going to inherit from my murder victim, I needed to talk to you. You understand, don't you?"

"Of course, Officer Barnes." She batted her eyes at him and I glared at her through the window. "I'm happy to talk to you. Whatever you need." She leaned forward, smiling, her low-cut top showing off her available assets.

"That's great. Thank you so much. You graduated from Baker Valley High didn't you?"

"I did. But unfortunately I was a little young to be there when you were. Not that I didn't go to watch your football games when I was in middle school, of course," she simpered before adding, "I was kind of sad to hear you'd gotten married this year."

I glared at her through the glass. Laying it on a bit thick, wasn't she? Of course, I had every faith that Matt knew how to play her right back.

He smiled at her, all warm and charming. "Well, when you know it's right, you know it's right. Was that how it was with you and Carl?"

"Oh, absolutely. I knew from the moment I saw him that my little Carl Bear was the one for me."

"How'd you meet? At work? Maggie and I met when I went to interview her for a murder investigation."

"Carl and I were the same. I went looking for a replacement gas cap and he and I got to talking and...I don't know. We just had so much in common."

Yeah, being murderous greedy psychos.

"When was that?" Matt asked.

"Gosh. The day after Luke's Fourth of July party, must've been? 'Cause I hadn't heard about Luke yet when I met Carl, but I know I hadn't met Carl at the time of the party because Luke and I were flirting a bit and I would've never done that if I'd already met my Carl Bear. We've been inseparable since we met."

"So you'd never met Carl before that day?" Matt asked, his tone suggesting that he knew she was lying to him even though I knew it was a bluff.

"Um." She tilted her head to the side. It was clear she wanted to say no, but she didn't quite have the guts to do it.

"Small town. Wouldn't be surprised if you had," Matt nudged. "You know, like me and football."

"Well, actually, I mean..." She tilted her head to the other side, smiling slightly, trying to be coy. "I guess that's why we knew so fast that we were meant for one another. Because we had met a while back. Even gone out a few times."

"Really? How'd you meet initially?"

She chewed on her lower lip. I'm sure it was supposed to be adorable, but it came off as nervous. "Ahhh...Online. One of those dating sites."

"Not a lot of local choices on those sites, is there?" Matt asked sympathetically, like he'd ever actually had to use one. The minute he came home every mother in the county with a halfway eligible daughter tried to set him up. "Which one did you meet on?"

"Sugar.ex."

"Sugar.ex? I've never heard of that one. Give me a second, let me pull it up."

She reached out and put her hand over Matt's. "No need. Really. It's, um..." She blushed and looked away. "It's a sugar daddy website? I wouldn't normally date an older guy like that unless, you know, he had something going for him?"

"Ah. A site for older guys with money and younger women?"

She nodded.

"So you thought Carl was wealthy when you met him?"

"He said he owned his own business and all. And the pictures he posted made it look that way."

"But you found out he isn't wealthy. And you ended it?"

She bit her lip again. "Basically."

"But now you're back together. And you even married him."

She nodded.

"What changed?"

She froze, realizing she'd probably made a mistake, but not quite sure what that mistake was.

"Does Carl have money now?"

She nodded again.

"How? Is he selling the business?" Matt asked.

"Mmhm."

"Why?"

"We thought we'd move. Find somewhere new to settle down. A fresh start."

Matt rubbed at his chin, leaning back. "I didn't realize Carl's business would sell for all that much.

Masonville Tire has been for sale for a year and I don't think he's had an offer yet. You sure Carl isn't putting one over on you?"

Addison ran her hand through her hair, agitated. "He's not. He has money now. He will."

Matt shook his head. "Hate to break it to you, Addison, but he's probably not going to have anything left after the sale of his business. He played you."

"No he didn't."

"I'm afraid he did."

"No. He didn't. I..." She pressed her lips together, no longer even pretending to flirt with Matt in her agitation. "Look. We weren't going to tell anyone about it because you know how weird people can be when it comes to money, but it turns out Carl's mom had won the lottery right before she died. He found the ticket going through her things."

"And that's why you got back together? Because now he's going to be worth something?"

"You make it sound so horrible. I liked the guy when I met him. I did.

But I don't want to be broke my whole life, living in some little town in the backend of nowhere. I needed someone who had prospects." She crossed her arms and leaned back in her chair, pouting.

"And Carl now has those."

"Exactly."

"And you found that out when you went into his shop for a replacement gas cap?"

She nodded.

"What day was that again?"

"I told you, the day after Luke's party."

"So Carl told you he was going to come into a bunch of money because of a lottery ticket the day after Luke's party."

"Yes! That's what I keep telling you."

Matt leaned forward, his gaze intense. I knew that look. I had been on the receiving end of that look. It was like having one of those bright lights they use to interrogate spies shining in your face. "Here's the problem with what you just told me,

249

Addison. That means that Carl was planning on that money being his before his mother was even dead. Which means he told you he was planning to murder her."

"No. What are you talking about? That's not what happened? I had the dates wrong. I must've met him after his mother died."

"That's not what he said in his interview. He agreed that you met the day after Luke died."

"I want to see him. I want to talk to Carl."

"Carl can't help you now, Addison. He has his own problems." Matt was all tough-nosed investigator now. I loved it.

"I want to see him." Her voice quavered, but her eyes were completely dry as she stared at Matt.

It was all just an act and Matt knew it. "No." He leaned forward. "Let me tell you what I think happened, Addison."

She crossed her arms and glared off to the side as he continued.

"I think you met Carl on that website, Sugar.ex, and he told you he was wealthy. Maybe you hit it off. Maybe you thought this was a guy you could like, assuming he really was as wealthy as he said. But then you found out the truth. That he didn't have any money. And you ended things. But then he contacted you. Or maybe you crossed paths at just the right moment. **Before** Luke's party."

Her eye twitched.

"He told you he had a way for you to be together. That if you'd just help him he could give you millions. He told you about the lottery ticket. That his mother and Luke were going to split the proceeds. He asked you to help him get that money. For the two of you. So you could be together."

She continued to glare off to the side, but her leg twitched under the table with each word Matt spoke.

"I bet if I look into your history I'm going to find a self-defense class. One that teaches kidney punches as a way to incapacitate an opponent fast. Am I right?"

A tear fell down her cheek. Finally, some real emotion.

"So what happened? You went to Luke's to kill him?"

"No! That wasn't..."

"The plan?"

She pressed her lips together and stared at Matt, clearly longing to say more, but not doing so.

He switched back to the soft, kind approach he'd started with. "Tell me what happened, Addison. I'll do what I can to help you." He reached across the table and squeezed her hand with his, keeping his attention focused completely on her, willing her to trust him. "I know you didn't want this. I know that's why you took those pills. You felt guilty for what you'd done. Tell me what happened and I'll help you as much as I can."

That finally broke her. She started to cry as she told Matt the truth. "I ran into Carl at the shop a few days before Luke's party. I don't know why I went there. I could've ordered that stupid gas cap online. But maybe I wanted to see him. I'd just broken up with some guy who was a total jerk and Carl had been nice to me. We started talking. And he told me about the lottery ticket and how he could finally give me everything I deserved. He said we just had to wait. His mom was elderly and frail. It would only be a matter of time. A few months? A year or two?"

"But..."

"But he said Lucas Dean had helped her buy the ticket and that she was going to give Luke half just for running to the store for her. That was money that could be ours. And she was just going to give it away to Luke. For what? Ten minutes of effort. He didn't deserve that. Carl said he'd tried to talk her out of it and she laughed at him. Said if he was a better son to her then he could've had it all."

"And then what happened?"

"I told him he should talk to Luke. Ask him to let go of his share. He'd understand."

(Yeah, right. Luke would've given up almost a million dollars because someone asked him to? No.)

"And? Then what happened?" Matt asked.

"We started hanging out. Carl and I. It was just a couple days. And then the day of that party I came home from work and he said he'd tried to talk to Luke. Said he went by Luke's and laid it all out for him. You know, how he was taking advantage of the generosity of an old woman who didn't know any better. But he said Luke just laughed. And said he had far better plans for the money than Agnes did. He said Agnes was going to donate half of her share to the Valley Fund. She wasn't even going to keep it. And if Luke gave up his share to her she'd just donate all of that to the Valley Fund, too." Addison looked at Matt, wide-eyed in disbelief as she recounted what Agnes had planned for the money.

He nodded sympathetically, keeping his gaze fixed on her. "What did you do next?"

She sank further into her seat. "I was...I was drunk. I'd been bartending and sometimes the guys like to buy me a shot, you know? I get better tips that way. And I just...When Carl told me what Luke had said, I got so mad. We were so close and now it was all just slipping away."

"So you went over to see Luke."

She rubbed her hands through her hair and then nodded. "I don't know what I was thinking. I had some notion I'd sleep with him and somehow convince him to give up his half of the ticket. Or..." She looked down at the table.

"Share it with you? Did you offer to leave Carl for him?"

She nodded, chewing on her lip.

"And? What did he say?"

She sighed as if her whole body was deflating. "Luke let me in, offered me a drink. We had a bit of a history, so he wasn't completely surprised I was there that night. I told him I'd heard he'd hit the jackpot and suggested he take me along. But he laughed at me. Said he already knew who he wanted to take with him and it wasn't some..." She sniffed back tears. "It wasn't some middle-aged washed out drunk. Told me nice try and to see myself out the door because he wasn't even interested in one last, you know."

Aleksa Baxter

"That's when you killed him."

She buried her face in her hands and sobbed, nodding her head in answer to his question.

"What about Agnes? Why did you kill her?"

She still had her face buried in her hands, so her answer came out mumbled, but it sounded like she said, "I didn't."

Matt reached across the table and gently tilted her head up.

"I couldn't hear you, Addison. What did you say?"

She sniffed back more tears. "I said I didn't kill Agnes, Carl did."

CHAPTER 36

According to Addison, she returned to Carl that night, freaking out about what she'd done, wanting to go to the cops and tell them. But Carl calmed her down and said it was all for the best. And then to show her that they were in this together he killed his mother.

He had Addison walk him through how she'd stabbed Luke so that he could use the same method. It took a couple days of practice before he was confident he could stab at the same angle that Addison had used.

The next night he waited until Patrice and her husband went to bed—which was sometime around eight-thirty—and then knocked on his mother's door claiming an emergency. When she let him in he killed her and took the lottery ticket.

To cement the deal Addison and Carl got married. The plan was to wait a couple more months before claiming to have found the ticket while organizing Agnes's papers.

Since they'd each killed someone, they were even, bound at the hip for eternity.

"Why tell me all this?" Matt asked when she'd finally run dry and was just sitting there, slumped in her chair. "You could've gotten away with it."

She shook her head. "I killed Luke in a moment of anger. I'd offered myself to him and he just laughed at me. But Carl...He was meticulous in killing his mom. Cold. He practiced for hours before he went over there."

She shuddered and rubbed at her arms as if chilled. "If I left here with him today, it would only be a matter of time before he decided to kill me, too. I figured it was better to be alive in prison, than dead."

I almost felt sorry for her. Almost. Until I remembered that she'd killed a guy because he didn't want to sleep with her and was rude about it and then helped a man kill his mother.

Carl, of course, refused to confess to his role in any of it. He called her crazy and screamed and ranted. But when they seized his computer they found internet searches on kidney strikes from before the date of his mother's murder. And there was a receipt showing that the date he and Addison reconnected was three days before Luke's party not the day after.

Also, good old Jolene and Patrice were happy to volunteer story after story of the horrible way that Agnes treated her son and how he was a little terror in the making. By the time they were done there was no doubt that Carl had built up years of hatred at his mother's cruel treatment and that he was more than capable of the killing.

I was overjoyed that we'd solved the case, but I couldn't take credit for it. I'd definitely played a part—there's no doubt that my information helped

Aleksa Baxter

move things along. But it was Matt
who was the hero of the day. I don't
think ninety-nine cops in a hundred
could've gotten that confession out of
Addison.

I was so proud of him. And I made
sure he knew it. Because that, too, is
part of being a good wife.

And one of the few parts that I
have no trouble fulfilling. My husband
is the best. I wouldn't have married
him otherwise.

EPILOGUE

On a gorgeous early August day I found myself at one of the most bizarre womanly rituals that exists on this planet: the baby shower.

Fortunately, Jamie had excused me from all future friend event planning duties after I'd miraculously saved her wedding day so all I had to do was attend. But it was like stepping into an alternate reality. A reality where every woman but me had either a baby bump or a child cuddled in her arms. There was even a woman breastfeeding right there out in the open for all the world to see, for crying out loud.

Not that there was a huge world to see it. Jamie's mom had set the whole thing up in her backyard and there were maybe twenty of us there.

Aleksa Baxter

But still. I did not need to see that wonderful act of nature, thank you very much. Just like I don't need to see other acts of nature. Pee, have sex, and breastfeed in privacy, please.

The whole backyard was decorated with stork-themed streamers and balloons and table cloths. It was like someone had vomited pastel colors all over the place.

And there were games. **Baby-themed** games. Like Bingo with squares for pacifiers and strollers and teddy bears.

That one I at least had a chance to win. (Although the prize was not a bottle of gin, sadly. It was a koala bib.) But the baby trivia? Oh no. There were literally women shouting over each other with the answers to the average length of labor and average new baby weight.

I suffered through, though, because this was my best friend we were talking about. But I finally hit my limit when a woman passed me what looked like a dirty diaper and asked me to smell it.

Turns out the brown substance in the diaper was melted chocolate and I was supposed to guess what kind it was. But no. No. No, no, no. You do not do that to chocolate. Especially not a **Krackel** bar.

I slunk off and stood at the edge of the crowd wishing I'd spiked my Coke with rum before I left the house.

Jamie found me there. She looked radiant in bright blue overalls over a yellow t-shirt. "Thank you for coming."

"I wouldn't have missed it for the world, you know that. I'm so happy for you." I gave her a quick hug.

She laughed. "I know you better than that, Maggie. This is the absolute last place you want to be."

"But I'm here for you. And I am happy for you. So happy for you. Just please, don't ever expect me to build you a diaper cake. That thing is…"

I glanced over to the side where there was a four-tiered "cake" made completely out of diapers and decorated with little baby toys. Whoever had taken the time to make that needed new hobbies.

Aleksa Baxter

(Look, don't get me wrong. I know some women love all of that baby stuff. I've seen them, I've met them. And if you are one of those women, good for you. But if you're not one of those women it's kind of like being surrounded by some baby-craving version of the Stepford Wives. You really are just waiting for someone to sneak you into a back room, knock you out, and inject you with a solution that makes you wake up yearning for a child or, better yet, ten of them.)

Jamie laughed. "It is impressive, isn't it? Maybe we can find a way to create a dog version for the barkery when it reopens. What do you think? Training pads and puppy toys?"

I tilted my head to the side as I studied it. "Actually, that's a really good idea. We could put a few stuffed animals around the base and a few chew toys on the upper tiers...Or dog treats. Ooh! Dog treats would work really well, wouldn't they?"

She grinned at me and I grinned back.

"You're going to have one mocked up before the week is out, aren't you?" she asked.

"Don't you know it. Speaking of, how's the ice cream project coming along?"

"Excellent. I made a pistachio cranberry caramel crunch ice cream that is to die for. You will love it."

As we stood there discussing Jamie's pregnancy-induced ice cream flavors and brainstormed more, I realized that I really, really was happy for her. She was going to be the best mother in the world, I just knew it.

And me? I was going to be the best adoptive aunt who drops by for short periods of time, never holds the baby until it reaches the non-breakable stage, and never, ever changes a diaper. (Because real diapers are not filled with melted chocolate, thank you very much.)

But what mattered was that we were both going to be happy in our own ways. (And murder free. Even if I had to kill someone to make that happen.)

ABOUT THE AUTHOR

When Aleksa Baxter decided to write what she loves it was a no-brainer to write a cozy mystery set in the mountains of Colorado where she grew up and starring a Newfie, Miss Fancypants, that is very much like her own Newfie, in both the good ways and the bad.

🐾 🐾 🐾

You can reach her at aleksabaxterwriter@gmail.com or on her website aleksabaxter.com